VINEGAR AND HONEY

By

JACK G. SALTER

To:

Teresa

First published by the Author 2009
All rights reserved
ISBN 978-0-9555169-3-1
Printed and bound in the U.K. by
Hobbs the Printers Ltd., Brunel Rd., Totton, Hants

This book is sold subject to the condition that it
Shall not by way of trade or otherwise, be lent,
Re-sold, hired out or otherwise circulated without
the publisher's prior consent in any form of binding
or cover other than that in which is published
and without a like condition including this condition
being imposed on the subsequent purchaser.

THE AUTHOR

Jack Salter was born in 1938 and educated at Hamble School. Following which he trained as an aircraft engineer at the former Air service Training Ltd. based on Hamble airfield. He also learnt to fly during this time.

He has held a number and variety of positions in industry and commerce, over the years, whilst flying, riding, piano music and writing have had the priority of his leisure time. And continues to this day.

He has two daughters and three grandsons and lives happily in retirement with his South African wife, Lincia, on the edge of the New Forest and continues to pursue his interest in the whole spectrum of aviation.

PROLOGUE

Vinegar and Honey is a story about a band of British commercial pilots, some might say, mercenaries, operating from Japan, some years after the Korean war came to an end. The pay is good but the flying errs on the dangerous side. The aviators not only have to contend with the vagaries of the firmament itself but also have to cope with the hazards that accompany aircraft, which are ill-maintained, fatigued through over-work and are, regularly, grossly over-loaded.

This tense, tooth-grinding account of the airmen gambling with their reputations and their very existence is set against the women in their lives and against a backdrop of an efficient, hospitable people, and a picturesque scenery, that is Japan.

ONE

In the pale light of the dawn the big jet swung onto the northern apron, and bowed to the lighted terminal building as the unseen pilot brought it to a halt. In the Arrivals lounge the PA system announced the arrival of the Oriental Express flight 912 from Tokyo.

A refuelling tanker and a host of servicing trucks converged on the big jet. Fore and aft hatches swung open. And presently the passengers began to stream out, smiling and paying their respects to the hostesses who had cared for them throughout the long flight.

Among them a young man, in his late twenties, dressed in a light brown suit, and conspicuous by his scarred face, thanked the hostesses for the pleasantries of the flight with a parting handshake, and made his way down the steps to head for the terminal building.

"I'm curious to know how he got those scars," a hostess remarked to her companion.

The other woman waited for a temporary pause in the disembarking passengers and said: "I don't think we'll ever know. He is bit of an enigma is our captain Dawson."

Her friend said, "But for his scarred face I could fall for him in a big way,"

The other woman said: "It takes courage to face the world as he does. I admire him for that alone."

The subject was interrupted by another surge of passengers spilling out of the hatch.

Dawson moved into the Arrivals lounge and secured himself a stale ham sandwich and a plastic cup purporting to contain coffee. He felt like an uninvited guest compared to his fellow passengers, milling around him, being greeted by excited, happy, smiling relatives and friends. Nobody, it seemed, had come to meet him in spite of the letter and telegram he had sent to warn of his homecoming. But then, he reminded himself, there were probably good reasons why they had stayed away.

He joined the coach for Victoria conscious of his scars drawing unwanted attention. He hid his face behind a newspaper and diverted his thoughts to Kimuko and the life he'd left behind in Japan.

From Victoria he went by taxi to Waterloo, got on a train for Southampton and swept himself out of view in the shadows of a corner seat in the buffet car. Gratefully nobody came to share the table. He was able to relax and sit and eat bacon and egg, toast and marmalade, and drink coffee, and watch the scene through the carriage window change from the closed-in, grimy architecture of the city to the wide open spacious greenery of the English countryside. Up against the skyline chequered fields rose and fell to the undulating geography. Isolated cottages and farmhouses nestled in pockets and hollows of the land. A meandering river, banked by wattle, fern and overhanging willow, reflected blue sky and small white clouds, which added to the magic and charm of the scenery. There is something special about the fresh green texture of the fields, the trees and hedgerows. He has never seen it in his travels abroad.

On arriving in Southampton he booked into a secluded hotel on the northern boundary of the town. He spent the first week arranging his finances, adding to his wardrobe and organising a hire car. He spent several sleepless nights debating how best he could deal with the situation whose outcome might very well cause a great deal of shock and distress.

Had it been his choice, and his alone, he would never have come back. But Kimuko had insisted he return to England to sort out his affairs and let the truth be known as a matter of courtesy to her and a mark of respect to his own family. For preference he would have let sleeping dogs lie.

Just over a year ago his next of kin had been notified of his death in an air disaster. Karen, his wife, requested his body be flown back to Britain. But the directors of Oriental Air Freight told her it was impossible because the machine had come down in a shark-infested sea.

Such lies had been fabricated to cover up the fact that Dawson and his second pilot were lost on a clandestine flight into China. What was more the airline could not produce a body and until the day Dawson returned to Japan nobody knew of his internment by the North Koreans.

The next dilemma for the airline concerned the pilot's facial disfigurement and mental scars from the tortures inflicted during his internment. He was in no fit state to be sent home to his family in England. He needed some attention to his face, and nobody in the airline were quite sure how to explain his reappearance to his relatives after they had been informed he had died in a shark-infested sea.

They rather hoped the pilot would take it upon himself to sort out the muddle for them. Instead, during the early weeks of getting back on his feet he struck up a friendship with a pretty Oriental girl, and committed himself to getting back on flying. He was in no hurry to go home to England, he told the directors of the airline; he was conscious of his scarred face and felt quite unable to explain to his relatives his return from the dead. There would be too much upheaval and confusion for him to resume the life there that he had led. He told the directors that it would be best for all concerned to let sleeping dogs lie.

Now back in England he could not bring himself to contact his relations; he put if off for another week. He visited his old lodgings in Hill lane to learn from a tenant in a downstairs flat that Mrs Garret had died. Her daughter-in-law, Ron Garret's widow, had inherited the house and continued to live in the midlands, and let the property out through a Southampton agent.

He drove to the centre of the town one evening and parked near a firm of solicitors and sat looking through the windscreen, smiling, and dwelling on memories of the first job he got when he moved down from the midlands. He saw desks and shelves crammed with soft covered files tied with green ribbon. He recalled with a smile the expression on the face of the old Barnaby, the senior partner, when he told him that it was his intention to get into aviation rather than pursue a future in the law profession.

During the following week, again delaying the contact with his relations, he drove out of Southampton and made his way to Hamble airfield. He parked in a lane on the boundary, reliving some of the moments he had spent at Air Service Training Limited where he had trained as a commercial and airline transport pilot. He thought of the many training flights he'd made by both day and night, in both single and twin-engine aircraft. His mind latched onto the many characters who had made up his fellow students and the ground and flying instructors. The airfield also reminded him of the many times he'd burnt the midnight oil studying for the all-important ground exams.

It had been a most rewarding and happy episode in his life.

He continued the visit by driving onto Hamble quay that also stored a host of memories. It was where he and Karen came and hired a rowing dinghy, in his leisure time, and made their way up river to the privacy of Badnam creeks.

He completed his visit to the village by calling in at the Coronation Arms, a public house, in which he had earned a few bob playing the piano in the public bar for a couple of evenings a week. It was where he and Karen had met for the first time.

It was fully a month before he plucked up the courage to contact his relations. He telephoned the Swanson's residence and for a good five minutes failed to convince James, the butler, who he was.

"Mr Gregory died in an air disaster." The old butler insisted. "No. I do not recognise your voice, sir." He paused. "Now if you must visit this residence it must be by appointment. Those are my orders, sir. What did you say the name is?"

"Dawson. Gregory Dawson."

"And who do you wish to make the appointment with?"

"Karen Dawson."

The old butler still refused to identify him. After a long silence he said:

"Very well, sir, would you be able to make it Thursday at 3.15."

Dawson confirmed that he could with a heavy sigh and wearily closed the line. More than ever he wished he hadn't come back.

* * *

He drove slowly along the laurel-sided drive to the Swanson's impressive home filled, as he was, with misgivings and trepidation. Even at this late stage he was tempted to call the whole thing off, fly back to Japan, and get Denver and King, two of the airline directors or the British Embassy to sort the mess out for him.

Too late! The butler was waiting between the pillars at the top of the steps of the main entrance and had spotted the car.

"Good afternoon, James." he greeted the butler with all the enthusiasm he could muster.

The old man's handshake was brief and limp. "I take it you are the Mr Dawson who made the appointment on Monday." he said very formally.

"That's right."

"If you would care to follow me, sir." He led the way inside, along the long high hall and stopped at the door of the drawing room.

"Somebody will attend to you shortly, sir. If you would care to step inside and take a seat. They won't be long. Now, you must excuse me."

The drawing room was not unknown to Dawson. He'd played the piano in this very room. He and Karen had announced their engagement here. And her father had refused him permission to marry her, very near the spot on which he was now standing.

He crossed the room to the baby grand piano, ebony bright, standing slightly to the left of the French doors. He smiled; he remembered its beautiful pitch and crisp clarity of note. And how it contrasted with the old Johanna he played in the pub at Hamble.

He recalled visits to the house by jazz bands and whose musicians were the favourites of Karen's father. Mr Swanson may have been a bit frumpy but he knew how to throw a good party. Dawson looked at his watch; how much longer had he to wait. Had he been forgotten or were they hoping he would tire and leave of his own accord.

After an incredibly long time the large oak door whispered open and Karen appeared. She put a hand to her mouth to disguise a gasp at the sight of his scarred face. She froze before him tall, slim, elegant, premature age lines on her brow and clutching at the corners of her eyes. Her hair was also turning grey. She was dressed in a laurel – green pleated skirt and a three-quarter-length suede coat.

"I'm sorry for everything being in a frightful mess," he said.

"Yes." she said. "It certainly is, isn't it."

She thawed a little and moved past him to stand before the French doors with her back towards him. He waited in the silence broken only by the pendulous ticking of a grandfather clock. Shadows moved across the glossy top of the piano: reflections of cloud passing a nearby window.

"When I received the first telegram," she said. "I refused to believe it. Not you, I said. It just wasn't possible. You were an ace in my eyes that took his flying seriously and never took undue risks. I went to bed each night thinking I would awake in the morning to find it nothing more than a nightmare. It went on for months much against mother and father's wishes who, in the end, had to take me to one side and, in no uncertain terms, tell me to stop dreaming and face the fact you were dead."

She turned to face him, the strain lines clearly visible. "But unknown to them, I continued to live in the belief that you were still alive. It was a struggle I can tell you and there were times I felt desperately lonely. Then I met Laurence at one of the house parties hosted by my parents. It wasn't an immediate attachment. He didn't rush his fences and possibly that is why I grew fond of him." She paused and looked at him as if checking his reaction.

"Go on." he invited her.

"Six months ago Laurence proposed to me. I got my marriage to you annulled. And as soon as the legalities were completed we were married."

He checked out of the hotel in the early hours of the next morning and headed north. Half way into the journey he was stopped by police and cautioned for speeding. They were very reasonable and courteous but being dark and the way they shone their torch beams in his face and the lonely spot in which they stopped him, triggered a spate of harrowing memories. He relived a terrifying and humiliating inquisition of the past. He saw evil faces with slanted eyes come out of the night to mock him. He heard piercing screams. His nostrils filled up with a nauseating stench of burnt flesh – human flesh – his flesh.

For a considerable time after the police departed he sat trembling like a leaf, sweating so profusely his vest and underpants stuck to him. Beads of perspiration ran off his brow, down over his cheeks and dripped off his chin. The salt in the perspiration stung the wounds upon his face.

As he sat smoking a cigarette the sweat began to chill. Composure came to him slowly. He got the car back on the road and turned the heating up full for a time, and continued the journey north.

He reached Rigby as dawn broke. He stopped the car on the crest of a hill and looked down at the town that rarely saw the full light of day because it lived under a permanent mantle of industrial smog. He recalled the days he had lived down there as a youth in a terraced house with a slate roof. He had a cramped bedroom at the back that looked out upon the lavatory roof, and further down in the small back yard there were rabbit hutches and pigeon lofts. He remembered that not a day passed without visits from neighbours who engaged his mother in local gossip and drank endless cups of her tea.

He had never felt at home up here. It was too drab and grey, too stifled, and people were too limited in their outlook on life. He had grown up surrounded by a local dialect and turn of speech that he had never quite understood. At school he was constantly ragged about his "posh" voice. He didn't know what that meant because he had always talked that way.

The only time he felt at ease was during his weekly piano lessons with Miss Methuen, his piano tutor. She spoke with a soft, gentle tongue and behaved as he thought a lady should. She never raised her voice in anger and, not once, did she get impatient with his difficulty in scale practice and sight-reading. The visit to her comfortable parlour was the highlight of every week as he sat in the flickering firelight, practising his music, and she plied him with tea and homemade cake.

He broke off his reminiscing to check the time. It was too early to call on his parents. He started the car, drove back down the hill and at the bottom turned left and headed out to the airfield some twelve miles to the east of Rigby.

The scene that greeted him was one of death and desolation; the airfield had been abandoned and was in an advanced state of decay. One of the main entrance gates had fallen off its hinges, its neighbour only needed a nudge and that would follow suit. He parked the car inside the gates and walked out on the tarmac apron before the hangar. Being an aviator the scene filled him with great sadness. The mast minus its windsock, the shattered windowpanes of the small control tower, the long, unkempt grass. He lit a cigarette and moved to the clubhouse whose untreated wood had faded and split. At one point the roofing felt had broken away from the apex and rolled down to the eaves. Somebody had made off with the main entrance door. He brushed aside a proliferation of cobwebs in the entrance. In the locker room one name had survived the neglect of the years – RON GARRET.

Dawson's thoughts flew back through the years to the tall figure of a flying instructor looming over him and saying, "It's no good thinking, young man. You must be positive and know exactly what you must be about if you intend to take up flying. Otherwise you'll end up wrecking more aeroplanes."

And Ron Garret it was who put him on the right road in life and helped get him away from the midlands. A truly great man!

Dawson moved further along the narrow corridor, treading on creaking floorboards, brushing aside more cobwebs, and came to the office of Mr Barnes, the club manager who he recalled as a short, balding man with a fiery temperament and a tongue to go with it. He had shown no mercy when he'd subjected Dawson to the most severe reprimand in his life and literally kicked his backside out of the door and out of a job, and without pay.

The pilot dusted a chair with a handkerchief and sat down. He drew on the cigarette and looked through a grimy window at the grass expanse of the airfield, and exhaled a long stream of smoke. His mind began to drift back through the years again. Gone was the uncertainty and awkwardness of his homecoming and the lingering nightmares of his tortuous imprisonment. They were episodes in his life which, as yet, had not happened.

Two

The take-off went very much as he expected. He pushed the throttle fully forward, the engine roared, and there was a combined surge of vibration and speed. He managed to prevent the nose swinging as he brought the tail up. The Chipmunk thumped along on the grass and, after letting it gain more speed he eased back on the stick and prompted it to take to the air. He drew a deep breath as it did so and the earth fell further and further beneath the wings. Over and down to the right the huddled buildings of Rigby disappeared beneath a grey blanket of smog.

At all costs he must not lose sight of the ground. He banked the Chipmunk on a climbing turn that took him onto the crosswind leg of the airfield circuit. Down at the tip of the tapering wing he spotted the diminishing size of the airfield and the toy like hangar, control tower and the clubhouse, outside of which an unusually large group of people had gathered.

At a 1000 feet he turned onto the downwind leg, eased into level flight and throttled back a little, growing ever conscious of his isolation and vulnerability; there was nobody in the rear cockpit to help him out if he got into trouble.

He turned and flew the base leg, throttling back a shade more but ignoring the use of the wing flaps; he wasn't quite sure how they worked. He promised himself he would never ever steal another aeroplane. If indeed there should be another time. He drew another deep, anxious breath.

He swung on to the final approach; he'd read a little about the technique of landing an aeroplane, but could claim no practical experience. A growing sense of helplessness seized him. The earth rose up slowly at first. Over the airfield boundary it came more quickly. In the last fifty feet it rushed up at him.

At first the spectators by the clubhouse thought he might make it. The boy was very popular amongst the club pilots and engineers, and was regarded as keen as mustard where flying was concerned. The machine came over the boundary going rather too fast. It rounded out and, with a combination of excessive speed and an over-correction on the controls, the machine climbed skywards with its nose at an acute angle.

"Get that bloody nose down! And go round again!" a voice bellowed in vain from the crowd.

The nose did go down – came level for a time and the Chipmunk seemed to pause momentarily in midair before it plunged earthwards unchecked. It hit the ground with a thunderous protest snapping both oleos, discarding the wheels and bending the propeller blades to half their diameter. The stricken machine travelled a short distance flattening the grass and gouging two furrows in the airfield surface with the sheared stumps of the undercarriage.

The boy looked up from the cockpit with the bewildered and despairing eyes of a rabbit caught in a snare.

Mr Barnes, the club manager, having lashed him with his tongue for a good ten minutes, lecturing him on the definition of trust, the respect and appreciation of other people's property and the perils of thieving, dismissed him on the spot and without any wages he was due.

His father had got him the job at the flying club and because they lived on the western suburbs of Rigby and the club was out in the sticks to the east his father had got him into lodgings near the club in a hamlet called Eastwood.

With the unrepentant words of Mr Barnes still ringing in his ears that evening the boy sat in his digs trying to unravel what he had done wrong on the disastrous flight and, at the same time, seriously considering what the future held in store for him.

He couldn't face going back to his parents. But most certainly he needed to get another job to keep a roof over his head and food in his belly. He would need references to get another job and he could not see Mr Barnes obliging on that point. All in all his life was in quite a pickle.

Voices on the stairs followed by tapping on his bedroom door was to reveal his landlady accompanied by Mr Garret, a flying instructor at the club.

"You've got a visitor, young Dawson. He wants to speak to you in private." the landlady said.

The boy thanked her, invited Mr Garret in and closed the door. He paused. Then furtively reopened the door slowly to ensure Mrs Clotter had returned down the stairs. The landlady was a kindly old soul but rather prone to snooping and eavesdropping.

"How are you feeling?" Mr Garret said.

"All right, thanks."

"Are you sure? You came down with a hefty bump this afternoon. You might have broken an arm or a leg. And did you hit your head?"

"No. I had the harness up very tight."

"I think you should let a doctor give you a check up."

"I'm not hurt. Really, I'm not."

The instructor regarded him with a smile. "What do you intend to do now that you've lost your job?"

"I don't really know. I was thinking that I should move right away from Rigby and start my life afresh where nobody knows me or my theft of the Chipmunk."

The instructor ruffled his hair. "It's no good thinking, young man. Whatever you do in life you must be positive. And you must also know exactly what you must be about if you intend to take up flying. Otherwise you'll end up wrecking more aeroplanes." He took a sealed envelope from an inside pocket of his jacket and handed it to him. "If you can find it in yourself to travel south to Southampton, go to the address on the envelope and hand it to my mother. I have asked her to care for you till you get back on your feet." He pressed a ten-pound note in the boy's hand. "You'll need that for the train fare. Now – when do you intend to leave."

"Possibly at the end of the week."

Mr Garret ruffled his hair again. "Don't dilly-dally. Be positive and do it. And promise me you won't go and bend any more aeroplanes." he grinned.

Dawson arrived at Southampton Central three days later on a dark, cold, wet, blustery evening. To save a taxi fare he waited for the rain to ease off before he walked from the railway station and made his way to the top of Hill lane, a solitary figure carrying a bulging, battered suitcase.

Mrs Garret lived in a rambling town house that had three floors and two attic rooms.

"So you are Gregory," she said after reading the letter from her son. "Come along in, young man, and get out of those damp clothes."

She lavished hospitality on him, inviting him to take a bath, treating him to a bacon egg and chips supper, and showing him to his room.

"This was my son's room." she smiled at him. "He insist you have it. He spent many an hour here studying for his flying examinations."

After she left he stood admiring his surroundings all so vastly different to that he had known up north. To start with the room was spacious with a high ceiling. There was a comfortable looking bed with a table next to it and a lamp with a warm, red shade. Against an adjacent wall a teak writing desk and chair. The next wall hosted a wardrobe. And to the left of the only window in the room was a chest of drawers. It took him a long time to digest the dramatic change in his circumstances.

The following day he was somewhat shocked when a GP came to the house, on Mrs Garret's instructions, and gave him a thorough medical examination.

"My son told me in his letter that you had been involved in an aircraft accident and took bit of a jolt," she said. "I gather nobody bothered to check if you had broken any bones or suffered other damage."

"It shook me up. But I'm all right otherwise."

"So the doctor told me before he left. But you are a bit pale, she said, and need a short rest and some solid food to build you up."

And so it was he settled in his new surroundings under her motherly care. He felt more at home with the southern people. He understood the dialect and they spoke a language less strident to those he had known up north.

Through her friends Mrs Garnett obtained work for him as a clerk in a local firm of solicitors. He found it all very staid and official and the décor and atmosphere verged on that of the Dickensian era. The wage was a fraction more to what he had earned at the flying club.

By the end of his first year with the firm it was quite obvious it would be many years before he saved enough money to finance the basic of flying courses. He got a job working at weekends as a petrol-pump attendant to boost his income. Then he answered an advertisement for a public house pianist, over at Hamble, for two evenings a week.

He cycled from Hill lane to Southampton Central and went by train to the little halt at Hamble, and pedalled down Hamble lane to the "Coronation Arms" the venue for his musical work.

There were no trains after closing hours at the pub. And therefore it entailed a long cycle ride home. But he was young and to him it was fun and he was earning money for it at the same time. He forged ahead quietly and diligently watching his savings grow.

A month before his second Christmas down south Ron Garret was killed in a freak flying accident. And as if the grief and shock of his passing wasn't enough for his mother it evolved that he had been making her an allowance to keep her afloat in the large house. His late father had paid off the mortgage but had no other funds to provide for her in his will.

Dawson suggested she took in more lodgers like him to cater for the shortfall in her income, and he would finance the necessary alterations to the rooms and the purchase of extra furniture. She said she would think it over when he put her on the train to go to her son's funeral and to stay with her daughter-in-law over Christmas.

He would have liked to attend the funeral with her but they were in the depth of winter and she asked him to stay behind to look after the house. Evidently the images of burst pipes haunted her.

Over Christmas, which he spent alone, he drew up plans for making the alterations to the rooms and looked through a telephone book for potential contractors to do the work and supply the furniture. He also decided where he would place an advertisement for lodgers.

New Year's Eve' found him out at Hamble entertaining the customers of the "Coronation Arms". By ten all three bars were packed solid with revellers. Cigarette and cigar smoke hung thick against the lights. Fumes of the ale and spirits drifted about in the incessant babble of conversation and regular bouts of boisterous laughter.

He worked unstintingly at the keyboard making music, some tunes of his choice, and others on request of the patrons who showed their appreciation by lining the top of the piano with pints of ale.

An hour before midnight he took a break. He downed two pints of ale, devoured a plate of ham sandwiches provided by the pub landlady, and accepted a cigar from somebody he didn't know.

He returned to the piano to the clinking of glasses and bodies jostling against the back of his chair. It was difficult at times to hear the music above the deafening bantering and celebrating going on around him.

Suddenly a hand came out of the crowd, handed him a folded piece of paper and, as quickly, disappeared. He continued playing with his left hand and unfolded the paper with his right. A message, which he thought to be in the hand of a woman, read: Please play for me, The Legend of Fujiyama.

He'd never ever heard of the piece; he was deeply suspicious. He smiled. Somewhere amongst the growing chaotic rowdiness about him an individual was mounting a private challenge to his skills as a pianist and musician.

With little prompting his fingers began to dance upon the keys as sketchy memories of school geography lessons submerged him in an atmosphere of the Orient. He saw Pagodas and Shrines. He walked along narrow streets crowded with rickshaws, and filled with the banter of Japanese women. He heard the strains of a samisen orchestra. He saw figures, in conical hats, tending the rice paddies, and the tea plantations. There was snow on the summit of the mountains. His fingers moved more urgently and pitched up the notes to describe an avalanche of snow. He saw an aeroplane flying near a mountain top. He saw figures in uniform wearing a red star on their uniform caps. He saw a face, a man's face, badly scarred and creased with pain. He captured the pain and transferred it to the music, with the notes rising to a screaming intensity.

The emotion slowly deserted him. His fingers slowed and softened their touch on the keys. Everything was calming down and he was aware that he was drawing the piece to its conclusion. He saw a young Japanese woman, dressed in a white kimono, standing on a small, rickety wooden bridge offering up, it seemed, her very soul to the revered Kami of Japan, mount. Fujiyama.

The impact of the music on the customers was quite overwhelming. A loud cheer went up, he received several thumps on his back in congratulations, and a hearty chorus went up for him to play it again.

He did so twice more, somewhat amused by his brief spate of fame. He wondered what Mrs Methuen would have thought.

At midnight the entire complement of customers joined arms and, heavy with sentiment, they almost brought the pub to its knees with a powerful rendering of "Old Lang Syne". A huge cheer went up and people shook hands or embraced in the process of exchanging New Year greetings. Dawson stood, looking on smiling and supping at his ale in between smoking a cigarette, occasionally having a hand thrust in his to thank him for the music and to wish him well for the New Year.

She appeared suddenly through a pall of cigarette smoke in the public bar, squeezing her way through the tightly packed crowd, a tall, slim girl with golden hair and cool, blue eyes. The crowd closed in behind her and catapulted her against him. He swung her around to a small space at the side of the piano.

"You took a gamble coming through that lot." he laughed.

She smiled and steadied her breathing. "Yes. My friends did warn me. But I was determined not to leave the premises without thanking you for the Legend of Fujiyama."

He caught the drift of her perfume. "You mean there is such a composition?"

"Shall we say there is now." she smiled.

He grinned back at her. "What was the idea behind it all?"

"We were listening to you in the lounge bar. And my friends disputed my claim that you were so good you could play anything. So, to prove my point, I sent you the title of a fictitious composition." She beamed her appreciation and temporarily held his hand. "Thank you for not letting me down." Her eyes strayed to the door of the bar where a hand was beckoning to her.

"I'm sorry. I'd better go. My friends are waiting." she smiled and touched his hand again. "And thank you once again."

Before she could make off into the crowd he took her hands and held them. "I'd like to meet you again." he said.

She pulled and pushed at his hands indicating she didn't want to go, but she must. She said quickly, "How often do you play here?"

"Wednesdays and Fridays."

A voice by the door bawled out her name and she was gone. He was certain he wouldn't see her again. A pity because he'd never had a close friendship with a girl before and, secondly, he considered her something quite special.

The following Wednesday the young woman put in a surprise appearance at the public house an hour before closing time. A group of men were playing dominoes. Three pairs were playing darts. Half a dozen stood chatting at the bar. Eyes turned as she tried unsuccessfully to make a discreet entrance.

"Hello again." she smiled warmly at him. "I hope I'm not interrupting."

He got up from the stool and shook her hand in greeting. "A welcome interruption if I might say. Can I get you a drink?"

She chose a tomato juice. He got that, offered her a ham sandwich from his evening ration and said, "Anything special you'd like me to play?"

Before she could answer a voice from the domino table said: "How about that one you played on New Year's Eve'."

"I played a hundred and one tunes on New Year's Eve', Fred."

"I nose yur did. But not as good as the one that sounded all ching-chong and chopsticks."

"Did it go like this?" the young woman played the opening bars.

"That's it!"

Dawson fetched her a chair. And together they shared the keyboard for the rest of the evening. She was far from being a novice. It needed a mixture of skill and cunning to get a decent tune out of the ancient, neglected pub piano. And she demonstrated that she was more than capable.

Following the closing of the public house they introduced each other and Karen insisted it was not an inconvenience when they secured his bicycle with bungie straps on the roof rack of her little Austin A35 and she drove him home to Southampton.

Two days later, on a Friday evening, much to his surprise and unending delight he discovered her waiting outside for him at closing time.

"Straight home? Or shall we go for a drive?" she said after they had put his bicycle on the roof rack.

He directed her up Hamble lane and into school lane and got her to park in a small space past a railway arch. He drew her attention to the night lighting of the airfield. From where they sat they were able to look between two tapering lines of flickering gooseneck flares which, he told her, marked the take-off and landing runway for the aircraft. A string of blue glim lamps dotted around the airfield helped guide the pilots to and from the runway. He pointed out to her the dim shape of a twin-engine Oxford waiting by the runway. Presently it moved to line up between the flickering runway flares. The engine note rose noisily and the machine surged away from them. Within seconds it clambered into the night sky discernable only by its white taillight.

The dark shape of her head against the moon-splashed window turned to him. "How long have you had an interest in aviation Greg?"

"As far back as I can remember." Beyond her window of the car another shape turned onto the flare path – and roared off into the night sky.

She took his hand. He had told her on Wednesday evening of his job with the firm of solicitors. "Wouldn't you like to get more involved with aviation?" she said.

On deciding she would have to know about it sooner or later he launched into telling her about his life up north, his misdemeanour of stealing an aeroplane and wrecking it. Then he told her about Ron Garret and his move south and all that had happened since.

Karen put a caring hand on the side of his face. "You poor dear. You stole an aeroplane." there was a hint of laughter in her voice. "You mustn't go through life holding that against you. We all make mistakes at some time or another. Including me."

He stirred and leant towards her. "I can't imagine you doing anything criminal, Karen."

She sat back in her seat and caressed his hand.

"It wasn't criminal possibly to the world. But it was to my family."

An aeroplane interrupted as it passed low over the car as a large shadow spurting blue and white plumes from its engine exhaust. In between the flares it plunged – checked itself – and fell noiselessly to earth.

"You see," she continued. "My parents wanted me to go to a finishing school in Switzerland. But I was more interested in horses. I was fed up with the classroom and had a burning ambition to start a riding school. So when it came to the entrance exams for the finishing school I purposely made a poor showing, and also left a very bad impression at the personal interview."

"Did it work?"

"Admirably. I now have my own stables which includes livery and I'm making, albeit, a small profit."

"You didn't actually steal anything from your parents."

"No. But I committed an equally serious crime, I deceived them."

They sat for a time in silence watching the silhouettes of aircraft come and go.

As she leant against him she shivered. After all it was January and without the engine running there was no heat in the car.

"I think we'd better head for my place and I'll treat you to hot chocolate," he said.

She started the engine of the car and she drove him back to Southampton where they ended up spending the night together and it seemed a perfectly natural thing for them to do.

Karen got home just after five next morning. She crept in through the tradesmen entrance and stole up the backstairs to her room. She bathed and changed and timed it to go down more or less the same time she expected her mother to appear.

She swept in to breakfast, "Good morning, mother."

"Good morning, dear." She noticed Karen had let her hair down and it tossed and swirled like the flowing mane of a young filly as she walked to the sideboard to serve herself breakfast. A warm glow filled her cheeks, her eyes sparkled, and her sweater and jodhpurs traced her youthful curvaceous anatomy. She was vibrant with energy and Mrs Swanson was in no doubt as to what was responsible.

They sat opposite each other at the long table. Karen tucked into a large plate of kidneys, bacon and grilled mushrooms and tomatoes aided by three tiers of toast.

"You look famished, my dear."

"Ravenous is more the word, mother."

"I didn't hear you get in last night."

"I was rather late."

"Did you go anywhere nice?"

"Only over to Hamble."

"With anybody I know."

Karen took a mouthful of food and delayed giving an answer until she had masticated and swallowed it.

"I met up with the pianist, mother."

"That's twice this week, isn't it?"

Karen nodded as she forked more food to her mouth.

Conscious of interrupting her daughter's meal she stopped further questioning.

"I've got some tidying up at the stables, mother. I'll be home at lunch time to help pack." Karen wiped her mouth with a serviette and left the table. They were going on holiday later that day.

Mrs Swanson moved to a window to watch her leave in her little car. She shook her head slowly. A mother's intuition told her that Karen had cast off all the trappings of a girl last night with the aid of the pianist. She remembered only too well the passions and the desires of her own youth, to condemn her daughter. But she was concerned that Karen might fall for the inevitable unwanted pregnancy: a stigma that her father, as a senior diplomat, could do well without.

The intimacy with Karen also brought a new impetus to Dawson's life. Whilst she was away with her mother on the skiing holiday, and before Mrs Garret got back he went ahead, without her agreement, and got the plumbers and fitters in to make the necessary alterations to make the vacant rooms into bedsits. He got secondhand furniture through ads in the local Echo. He got the office to draw up tenancy agreements, at a reduced price, and in which it was stipulated that the rent would be paid by a bank standing order so as to spare the landlady from chasing her tenants for the rent. He placed a small solitary advert for tenants, in the Southern Evening Echo and the telephone did not stop ringing for three days.

A day before Karen and Mrs Garret were due back he was summoned to the office of Mr Barnaby, the senior partner in the firm of solicitors.

"I am given to understand by various members of staff that you are demonstrating quite some flair for legal work, Gregory. And they think, as do I, that you should consider attending evening classes with a view to obtaining a legal qualification."

Dawson thought quickly; the job was important to him as a source of income and he didn't want to disappoint Mrs Garret who had pulled the strings to get him the job in the first place. He chose his words carefully,

"I do enjoy the work, sir. But I must be honest with you and admit I am more interested in something which is quite remote from law."

The distinguished old gentleman grinned at him. "May I ask what it is?"

"I hope eventually to get into aviation."

"A commercial pilot, I take it?"

Dawson nodded.

Barnaby formed an apex on his desk, elbows spaced, hands clasped "The training is expensive, is it not?"

"Several thousand pounds from what I know."

"Is it possible to achieve it on a clerk's wages?"

"I have other work to help me along. I play the piano two evenings a week, and work as a petrol pump attendant at week-ends." He mentioned nothing about the savings he had spent on Mrs Garrret's house.

Barnaby stood. "Very well, Gregory. It's a pity you don't see a future in law for yourself. But, at the same time, I admire you for your honesty, and the enormous challenge you have set yourself."

Dawson said quickly, "Do I still have a job here, sir?"

"Yes, of course. Keep up the good work and you are welcome to stay as long as you like."

In February that year it turned very cold and brought snow. It fell all night and by morning it was so deep it almost brought the country to a halt. More significantly it stopped him and Karen meeting; he wasn't prepared to risk her driving all the way from Hill Head to Southampton, in such treacherous conditions, and all the way back at night. They kept in contact by telephone and sending cards to each other. For nearly a month he was unable to get out to Hamble to play the piano. He managed to keep the petrol pump job going.

He trudged home from the office through the deep snow, of a Friday evening, slipping and sliding through the big drifts. The wind blew up station road like a chilled knife blade cutting through the thickest of clothing and swiping at his exposed face. Half way down the hill a town bus began to swing in the road. By the time it reached the bottom of the hill it was facing back up the hill. A number of passengers opted to join him on foot and walk up Hill lane.

To combat the chilled air he diverted his thoughts to pondering on what Mrs Garret had prepared for his evening meal. He would have a leisurely bath, telephone Karen, and take an early night, he decided.

He found a letter by his side plate at dinner. He waited for Mrs Garret to serve him a bowl of Scotch broth before he recognised a symbol on the envelope as that of his Bank. He turned it over a number of times debating on what the letter might contain; he'd put through some hefty cheques for the refurbishment and conversions of the rooms. He had double-checked his arithmetic and was convinced he had been left with a small balance.

He waited for Mrs Garret to come and take the empty soup bowl away before he decided to open the envelope, feeling quite dubious as he did so. He undid the three folds in the single sheet of official notepaper. Very gradually his serious expression relaxed, his eyes opened wide and his mouth dropped open in surprise.

Dear Mr Dawson,

I write to advise you that an individual who wishes to remain anonymous has deposited a sum of money to your account.

I have been instructed to tell you that the money is to be used strictly for flying lessons. And I trust you will furnish the necessary evidence as, and when, you embark upon your flying training.

Yours sincerely,

B. Inskip

THREE

Hamble airfield played host to Air Service Training Ltd., an organisation, renowned throughout the world, for its outstanding quality and style of training to fulfill the international needs of aviation. Students arrived there from all corners of the globe to train as pilots – navigators – radio operators – ground engineers. Few, if any, would ever leave, at the end of their training, without happy memories of the time they spent there upon the airfield, in the workshops and hangars, the lecture block and the comfortable living quarters.

Many students forged a lasting friendship amongst the complement of professional and friendly ground and flying instructors. A number found a future wife in a local village girl.

The airfield nestled in a crutch of land formed by Southampton water and the river Hamble. And in addition to the contingent of civil training aircraft the airfield accommodated a number of military training contracts.

In the 1950s the flying programme could cover eighteen hours a day, and the air above and around Hamble village was a scene of arriving, departing and passing aircraft and the incessant drone of their engines that went well on into the night. None of the local residents complained; it was all considered as part and parcel of village life.

It was to this homely country setting that Dawson arrived as a fee-paying student to train for his commercial and airline transport licences for the next three years.

He trained on single and twin-engine aircraft gaining experience on both by day and by night. He flew long cross-country flights to sharpen his pilot navigation skills. He was taught to fly on instruments.

On the ground he was regularly in the lecture block furthering his knowledge on aerodynamics, principles of flight, aircraft structures and power plants, navigation plotting, meteorology, aviation law and weight and balance procedures. And when he wasn't in the air or at a lecture he studied the numerous subjects late into the night. It was a tight course but he thrived on it.

He enjoyed every moment he spent at Hamble, which was complemented by Karen's friendship and her support and enthusiasm for his studies.

During the summer months she would make up a picnic basket and they would hire a small clinker-built boat and he rowed it up Hamble River to a secluded spot amongst the creeks below Badnam copse. The first occasion was made memorable by the fact he had never handled a boat before. But he soon learnt after initially going round in circles for a time much to the amusement of a number of onlookers.

They moved up river, Karen leaning back in the stern of the boat, eyes closed, with each of her hands dragging in the water on either side and he fought to synchronise the movement of the oars. They passed between many buoyed yachts till they got up river and turned into the creeks. And it was at that very moment, the sun caught her at a certain angle, dissolving her yellow, red pin-striped summer dress, and gave him an unobstructed view of her young firm, rounded breasts, the small coil of her navel and the small dark triangular shadow that marked her modesty. She later revealed she had abandoned her underwear.

In the winter months they might go for a quiet drink, or they'd meet after he'd done his stint on the piano in the Coronation Arms; it gave him a few bob for his pocket. Sometimes they visited Mrs Garret. Karen often treated him to a meal in an inexpensive restaurant. A number of times they went dancing at the Guildhall in Southampton. On rare occasions they pooled their resources, drove down to Bournemouth, and booked into a hotel for the night.

Henry Swanson crossed to the cocktail cabinet and mixed a whisky and soda for himself, and poured a sherry for his wife. "Do you know, my dear. I've been home a fortnight and have barely seen my daughter. She is either too busy at the stables, or, she is dashing off to some social event," He turned to her, drinks in hand. "Perhaps you can enlighten me. Is she still liaising with this solicitors' clerk – this public bar pianist?"

"Don't be too hard on her, Henry. Or the boy for that matter."

He sat down beside her, a troubled expression masking his face. "But is he in our class, my dear? You know what I mean – my position within the foreign office and my reputation where the government is concerned."

She patted his knee. "They are young and very much in love. Romantically adventurous just as you and I were at that age."

"But you and I came from similar social backgrounds." he sighed heavily. "It wouldn't be so bad if this boy was something more than a clerk or a dabbler in public house music."

She patted his knee again. "Henry Swanson – you can be quite a snob at times. You also have a habit of judging people in the absence of all the facts."

"I'll have you know, my dear, I have always been considered as something of an expert on the subject of character analysis."

"Well – you are quite wrong about this young man, Henry. The latest news from Karen is that he is training at Hamble to become a commercial pilot."

A month before what would have been his third Christmas at Air Service Training LTD Dawson had sat his ground exams, undertaken his general flying tests, and obtained his flying licences. To celebrate his success Karen booked them into the Vine at Ower for a candlelight dinner and dance. His only regret was that he was unable to thank the generous anonymous person who had donated the finance for his flying courses. He tried to prise it out of his Bank but they point-blank refused to name names.

Karen had assured him she was not guilty. So it basically came down to Mrs Garret or the old Barnaby at the solicitors. But Mrs Garret's delicate financial position ruled her out. And would a solicitor invest in something like aviation, and in particular invest in somebody from whom he was unlikely to get any return. It was very doubtful.

He didn't seriously think his parents up north would do it. They weren't that flushed for money and for certain he had disgraced them by stealing the Chipmunk. Barnes, the club manager, would have obviously have told them and, knowing him, he probably suggested they should pay something towards the damaged he'd caused. What was more he had not kept in touch with his parents after the incident at the flying club because he felt too embarrassed?

He finally concluded he would probably go through life never knowing and that was a great pity.

Most students at Air Service Training LTD were Government or Airline sponsored and therefore had a job to go to when they finished training. Others like Dawson had to make their own way into aviation. He decided, and Karen agreed, that he should take a short break and start looking seriously for flying work in the New Year.

He moved back in with Mrs Garret and he looked after the house again that Christmas whilst she went up north to her daughter-in-law. The landlord of the Coronation Arms twisted his arm, and New Year's Eve' found him at the piano.

As soon as the New Year was in Karen collected him from the public house and drove him to her home in Hillhead to meet her parents, a promise she had made to her father. Dawson noted with interest the long drive that led to a large white Georgian style building which seemed to have a light at every window. Cars lined both sides of a long gravel drive that led to the semi-circular complex facing the steps leading up to the main entrance. French doors had been thrown open and a combination of piano, saxophone, clarinet, trumpet and drum sent out a cheerful, colourful jazz composition together with clouds of cigar and cigarette smoke to the chilled, clear night air.

The party that had started at eight was still in full swing. Dawson lost count of the guests Karen introduced him to. He met and spoke for a time to a gentleman farmer, an insurance broker, a solicitor, and a school headmaster, James, the family butler, and an amusing Harry Soil, the family gardner.

Mrs Sawson took to him immediately. But Karen's father received him with a polite, cautious detachment.

Rather conveniently at this time the band left their places for a break and Karen asked Dawson to take to the keyboard and play the Legend of Fujiyama as a special request of her mother.

Murmurs of conversation, and pockets of laughter faded when he was only a few bars into the introduction. Figures hurried from other rooms and the patio and crowded into the room to listen.

Dawson was both intrigued and puzzled each time he played the piece. It came easily from the cloisters of his memory and flowed through his fingertips onto the keys. But each time he played the same succession of scenes passed before his mind's eye. It always started with a formation of quaint pagodas, narrow streets, chattering Oriental voices and the plaintive notes of a samisen.

Then he saw an aeroplane flying by the snow-capped peak of what he thought to be a mountain.

Next he was confronted by sinister looking figures dressed in uniform with distinctive red stars on their caps. And following on from this he was confronted with a scarred face that filled him with pain and anguish.

The turmoil in his mind only began to recede as he drew the piece up to its conclusion. It was when he always saw a young Japanese woman, dressed in a white kimono, standing on a wooden rickety bridge offering up, it seemed, her very soul to the towering Mount Fujiyama.

He always felt the music and scenes were trying to tell him something. But he repeatedly failed to interpret what it was. He'd never been in the Orient; in fact he had never stepped off English soil. It was all rather bizarre.

In the New Year he got down seriously to looking for work in aviation. He bought a bundle of the relevant magazines and started combing the Situations Vacant columns and sending off for application forms. He wrote to several flying enterprises that were not looking for aircrew; he thought that by showing an interest in them they might be goaded to show an interest in him. He also telephoned a number of companies.

A few companies replied to him; a great number did not. Then he began the next part of the exercise by filling in, and sending off the application forms, twelve in number. And waiting patiently for a response.

By the fifth week he was feeling quite dejected. His attempts to get into flying, ended with three companies saying he lacked experience for the position they had on offer. Another three suggested he needed more hours on his log book, and the remaining six said the position had been filled but they would put his name on their list for future vacancies.

He went, cap in hand, to the old Barnaby at the solicitors and the diplomatic gentleman, that he was, found him some clerical work with a reasonable wage. He also went back to playing permanently at the Coronation Arms, two evenings a week, and working the petrol pumps at weekends for a couple of shifts.

After three long months of suppressed anguish and frustration at being denied access to the flying scene, he came across it as he thumbed idly through an aviation magazine one evening.

COMMERCIAL PILOT WANTED FOR BUSY
SUMMER SEASON IN BLACKPOOL. GOOD
OPPORTUNITY TO BUILD HOURS.

He jumped to Mrs Garret's hall telephone and dialled the number on the advertisement, hoping desperately it was not too late in the day.

The line opened to an abrupt midland accent, confirming the number.

"According to Aviation Monthly you urgently want a pilot for the summer season. And I desperately need a job." Dawson said a little breathlessly.

"You do, do you. Right! Let's have some details."

After giving his name, address, age and his training at Air Service Training Ltd. the voice at the other end said, "What twin did you fly at Hamble?"

"The Airspeed Oxford."

"So you think you could handle an Avro 19?"

"It's more placid than the Oxford from what I know."

After a pause and the sound of papers being shuffled the man said, "Right. It's fifty quid a week plus a bonus and free digs. But if I find your tickets or medical out of date I'll send you away with a flea in your ear. Understood?"

"I won't let you down."

He thought he heard a quiet chuckle at the other end before the man said, "You'll need to do minor maintenance on the kite. Okay?"

"That's all right by me."

"Good. When can you start?"

"As soon as you like."

"Let's make it a couple of weeks from now. And phone me a couple of nights before you come so that I can pick you up from the station."

"Fine."

"One more thing. Do you like hard work?"

"Love it."

"You're a fool to say it," the man chuckled. "But then I like employing fools. See you in a couple of weeks. Cheerio."

The work in Blackpool consisted of giving pleasure flights to a multitude of holiday visitors in a rather overworked and neglected Avro Anson 19 whose port engine was abnormally thirsty on oil, and its starboard tyre needed to be topped up daily with air. Apart from that she had no serious vices and she plodded on day after day without complaint?

Dawson shared the piloting with Harry, an older man who had flown a Lancaster during the war and who had no wish to talk about it. They flew a ten-hour day, split into two shifts, a late and an early, and rotated the shifts on alternate weeks.

Jimmy Roebuck owned and managed the enterprise known as Midland Aerial Services Ltd. The company had a board of 3 directors and the equivalent number in employees.

Roebuck, a short, comical character had the gift of the gab and knew instinctively how to make a fast buck. He could cajole the most nervous of earthlings into the air, some of whom didn't get much of a chance. He bundled them into the aeroplane, showed them to a seat and strapped them in, thrust a sick bag into their hand, and told them to hold on tight and enjoy the flight. And before they could change their mind he was out of the aeroplane, slamming the door shut, and signalling to the pilot to get a move on.

Brakes off – open the throttles to get under way – and carry out the take-off checks en route to the runway. A call to the tower for clearance and swing onto the runway and run forward to straighten the tail wheel. Then its full power and the Anson pounds along the runway in the roar of its Cheetah engines. It's an exhilarating experience, not least of all for him, the pilot, using his commercial flying licence for the first time. His left hand holds the control wheel, his right grips the engine throttle levers, his feet rests on the trembling rudder pedals his eyes switching back and forth between the view through the windscreen and the instrument panel.

A steady heave on the wheel and they take to the air. Their passage becomes smooth and the frantic roar of the two engines steadies and lessens as he adjusts the boost and revs. Their climbing flight becomes a magical experience threatened, as it is occasionally, by an unsettling decision of the aeroplane to zoom or plummet in patches of hot, summer turbulent air.

Fortunately for many of the nervous passengers the flights are not of long duration. The machine carries them up and around on a loose circuit of the aerodrome, and half way round it starts the descent back down and around onto the final approach, a flight of little more than twenty minutes.

The weather that summer was ideal. The sun shone perpetually from a dazzling blue sky and the rare visitations by cloud came in small armadas of fair weather cumulus. The pilots flew in shirt sleeves and sunglasses and used the air vents to the full. The Avro 19 behaved impeccably despite the splits in her fabric skinning, and the scratches and growing number of oil streaks from loose rivets on the engine cowlings.

He got up at six on a typical morning shift. He lived in a boarding house recommended by Roebuck and helped himself to breakfast from a table laid out by the landlady the previous evening. There was grapefruit, an assortment of cereals, and a jug of milk and bread he could toast on the oven grill. If he felt inclined and had the time he could fry bacon and egg and black pudding and heat up tinned plum tomatoes.

Roebuck also gave him the loan of a bicycle as a means of transport to get to work which involved a twenty-minute ride. The exercise compensated much for the long hours he spent sat in the cockpit of the Anson.

On arriving at the aerodrome he gave the aeroplane a thorough pre-flight inspection, always finding it necessary to get hold of a portable compressor to top up the air in the starboard tyre, and the air in the pneumatic wheel brakes system. Then he ran and got the engines up to working temperature.

The joy riders normally started queuing at half eight and Roebuck greeted them with a request to pay up and look big for their forthcoming adventure. He got the first lot strapped in their seats. Then he hurried round and disconnected the starting trolley after the pilot had started the engines. He gave a brisk wave of an arm as a signal to the pilot to get a move on. Then he turned and rubbed his hands; more joy riders were forming a long line; he was going to make a few bob today.

The pilot finishing the late shift refuelled and oiled the Anson and generally tidied the cabin so that flying could start promptly the following day. Dawson normally finished the shift with a cigarette and a long glass of chilled lager and lime in the aerodrome bar and, whilst he was about it, he wrote and sent Karen a postcard.

He flew every day for twelve weeks. The daylight hours began to shorten and the bookings dwindled overnight.

"That's it. Finito!" Roebuck announced one particularly quiet day. "I'm not sending the aeroplane aloft half empty. It eats into my profits."

Dawson left Blackpool with his wages barely touched plus a modest bonus and nearly an extra five hundred hours on his logbook. Roebuck for all his market trader style of doing business had given him his first break in commercial flying; he'd always be grateful to him for that. In addition there had been the loyal and forgiving nature of the Anson that had never let him down.

He remembered the last time he saw her at the aerodrome when he went down to collect his pay and bonus. She stood on the tarmac outside a hangar, sagging at the undercarriage and showing the signs of her twelve weeks of uninterrupted flying. Paint had flaked off her metal and fabric surfaces in several places. There were numerous splits and cracks in the fabric. A growing pool of oil had formed beneath the port engine. The starboard tyre was very nearly flat.

The good news was that Roebuck had sold her to a survey company that had booked her in for a major overhaul.

The journey back south by train was a profoundly happy one. He had the carriage to himself and as he sat watching the passing scenery, and idly reflected on events of recent months, he felt smug and rather proud. Life had been good to him. It had not only given him an opportunity to fly every day but in the bargain he had been paid for it. Honey days, he murmured. Days when everything went right for him and compared to the time he moved south to start a new life, and the unknown person who paid for his training at Hamble.

The other days, the bad days, he regarded as the vinegar days. Such as the life he'd led up north, the incident with the Chipmunk and the tragedy of Ron Garret's death. Then those three whole long months trying to get work in the flying scene. Those were certainly the vinegar days.

Within days of returning to Southampton and carried by his successes in Blackpool he bought a secondhand car and taught himself to drive on a stretch of road leading to Southampton Common.

He phoned Karen of an evening and gave her the impression that he was still up north. Next day he had the car filled with petrol, and took the plunge. He ventured through the town traffic and headed out on the country roads to Hill Head and her stables.

As he pulled into the yard her curious expression exploded into laughter and tears when she recognised him. She handed the horse, she was attending, to one of the girls and hurried to the car. He put a hand on the door to stop her opening it. "Good afternoon m'lady." he said. "This is your new Rolls. And I am your new chauffeur. Pilot is the name."

She ran a hand along the roof. "It's great, Greg."

"It ought to be m'lady. It cost your father a fortune. He has instructed me to take you for a spin to ascertain if you approve of the model." He clambered out, warding off all her attempts to embrace him, and made his way round to the nearside door. "Would her ladyship kindly enter the limousine."

"But Greg, I'm all grubby." she protested.

"A faint hum of horse manure, my lady, which I suggest will make the engine run more harmoniously."

"Greg," she pleaded with him. "Do you realise it is over three months since we.... I'm ravenous"

"M' lady, " he continued the pretence. "The master has warned me of the perils of conniving with her ladyship. Now, I must insist you enter the limousine."

She finally relented. And in the sound of noisy tappets, and trailing a cloud of blue smoke the polished Ford Poplar moved from the stables and turned out on to the road for Fareham.

"Where are we going, Greg?"

"A test drive, m'lady."

"Very well. But don't stop. Just look at me," she plucked at her clothes. "Muck on my boots, torn jodhpurs and a sweater full of holes."

"You forget the hay sticking out of your ears. A picture of rare beauty, if I may say, m'lady."

Five miles on he pulled into a side street and parked the car and when she refused to get out on account of her appearance he lifted her out bodily and would have carried her to the High Street had she not agreed to walk.

She hid behind him as they made their way past numerous shops and pedestrians and eventually came to the window of a Jeweller. He drew her alongside him, put an arm around her and said, "It would please me greatly if her ladyship would accept an invitation to choose an engagement ring."

Karen's delighted mother put on a small party to celebrate the occasion. A four-piece was laid on and twenty guests were invited. At the height of the evening Dawson went through the motions of asking for a private audience with Karen's father at which he requested his daughter's hand in marriage.

The diplomat looked at him over the bowl of his pipe to which he was holding a lighted match. He got the tobacco burning and blew a stream of smoke toward the ceiling, "Let me begin by saying that I do approve of your relationship with Karen, Gregory. But with the greatest of respect I don't think marriage would be wise in your present circumstances…"

"But…" Dawson interrupted.

"No, I'm sorry. Let me finish." the diplomat said firmly. "You too may have a daughter in the future who you'll treasure as much as I do Karen. And like me you will want only the best for her. Now – let me ask you three questions. Number one. Are you employed at the moment?"

"Not exactly."

"Number two. Could you finance a stylish wedding?"

"At a pinch."

"Number three. Have you considered where the pair of you would live?"

" Not really."

Swanson drew on his pipe and exhaled a cloud of smoke, "Then be honest, young man, and admit this is not an opportune time for you to embark on marriage. Get yourself firmly established on an airline with a reasonable and regular income, and own a property that reflects my daughter's background, and I promise to give my consent."

Four

Just over two months from the day that the couple got engaged Dawson was working a pick and shovel under the sweltering sun in Australia at the erection site of a hydroelectric plant. Having been driven, in part, by Karen's father's attitude, and partly because his prospects for getting into aviation, in Britain, looked bleak. The British press claimed Australia was the country of the future offering boundless opportunities and this, in turn, invited the suggestion there would be greater openings in the flying business. It was a wrench leaving Karen behind but he booked his passage and she, tearfully, saw him off, from Southampton, in the company of her mother and Mrs Garret.

Within days of arriving in Australia the Bureau of Employment told him the glowing opportunities, bandied about in Britain, was nothing more than a puffed-up publicity stunt. And that there were 4000 pilots out of work. Quite frankly you don't have a hope in hell, he was told.

"Why not try legal work." the clerk drawled. "Your application form says you worked in a solicitors office. And we could do with some law clerks."

Dawson said: "What other work do you have?"

"Plenty of office wallahs. Book-keepers, salesmen and the like."

"What about open-air work?"

"You talking about construction work?"

"Yes."

The clerk raised his eyebrows in surprise. "You wouldn't get a look-in with hands like yours, digger."

"Let me be the judge of that." Dawson reprimanded him.

The clerk fell silent, picked up another file from his desk, and thumbed through it. After a while he withdrew a sheet from the file and handed it to Dawson. "They need hands up at Lakebed creek. They say the work is lousy. But the dough is good."

"Where and to whom do I apply?"

The clerk ringed a name on the sheet. "You'll find them on the third floor in this building. Tell Bert Morgan I sent you."

Morgan was as tall and broad as a barn door. His face had the complexion of a walnut and his speech was heavily traced with the Anglo-Saxon language.

He was outspoken to the point of being insulting. He ended his interview by saying, "You don't look the type for the sort of work, Pommie. But I'll give you a try. You'll meet diggers who hate your guts. Take my tip, ignore 'em and you shouldn't have any problems."

And so it was Dawson duly arrived at Lakebed Creek and committed himself to the rugged life amongst the good, bad and indifferent types who made up the work force.

He did not find the pick and shovel work overly demanding. In fact it improved his physique and the exposure to the sunlight bronzed him to a point Karen could not quite believe it was him when he sent home the first lot of photographs.

Social life on the site hardly existed. The main contractor flew in a bounteous supply of beer on a frequency with the weekly visit of the mail plane. Apart from that there were some blue movies which, in the main, were ignored. Someone got to hear that Greg Dawson dabbled in music and Morgan had a piano transported to the site. Henceforth he was regularly in demand.

But for him the highlights in his life on the desolate site were the letters from Karen. He sent her a money order each month to put into a joint account. He told her they would have enough money for a good wedding, and to buy a house when he returned home in the Spring. She wrote him long intimate letters in return saying she couldn't wait to get him home, and she wouldn't be parted from him ever again.

He was on the verge of going to the site recreation hut to play the piano for the New Year celebrations when he bumped into Hog Patterson. They were about to pass when Hog stopped and said, "Hey Daw. Yur a flapper ain't yu?"

"Of sorts, Hog. Of sorts."

"Well, I was in Kollawonga yesterday and there was this yank looking for guys to fly his ships as he called 'em."

"Did he mention what ships they were?"

"I think he did. But I can't remember. I know he said he only wanted peelos – not cowboys."

"Did you catch his name?"

Hog screwed his eyes up and frowned heavily as he attempted to resurrect his memory. "Denby – Delby – nah. It might have been Denver. I can't rightly remember. He's shacked up at Drydust hotel. That I know."

By the end of the first week in January Dawson was sat in a back room of the Drydust hotel before the bloated figure of Denver. He had hitched a ride to Kollawonga in the Cessna mail plane and the pilot promised to fly him back to the site for the price of a taxi fare.

The American was not a man to be trifled with. He knew precisely what he wanted and gave the impression he always got what he wanted. For a considerable time he inspected Dawson's log book and licences. Dawson had a horrible feeling he was going to say his 500 hours at Blackpool were not enough. Instead the American lit a long cigar, leant back in his chair and said, "My outfit operates from Japan and we use C47s, DC3s, 4s and 6s, a C119 Packet plus a

PBY amphibian. We don't work set hours and you'll fly anywhere and at any time the ops manager tells yuh. Yuh never question what yur carrying, and just query the dollars we pay yuh, if you get the time. The ships are rarely serviced. It's up to yuh to nurse 'em along. Think yuh can handle it?"

Dawson ignored the question and said, "What is the life expectancy of your pilots, Mr Denver?"

The American roared with laughter. "Life expectancy! I like it man. It's real cool." He likewise ignored Dawson's question and said, "Tell me, Dawson. Do yuh drink?"

"Well – let's put it this way I don't believe in dehydration, if that's what you mean."

"Come off it yuh clever bastard. I'm talking about the hootch – the fire water."

"From what you say there won't be time for sleeping let alone going on a binge."

"The point I'm trying to make." Denver said seriously. "Is that I get real fussed up with piss-artists. There's no room for them in my outfit. We carry expensive cargo for customers who carry a lot of weight in the Orient. Lose them and we are out of business and yu are out of a job. Yuh get me?"

Dawson nodded.

Denver said: "When can you start?"

"My contract says a month's notice."

"What's the name of the boss man on site?"

"Bert Morgan."

"I'm returning to Japan at the end of next week and I want yuh on that flight. Even if I need to grease a few palms."

The long jaunt to Japan was to provide an accurate picture of how Oriental Aerial Freight conducted their affairs. The DC6 had been stripped of seats and upholstery to accommodate fuselage fuel tanks to give the aeroplane its range. The conversion had been done in a hurry: evidence of which was shown by ragged hanging bits of the disturbed upholstery, and fumes from the fuel drifted unchecked to the flight deck. Denver regularly left the flight deck, spanner in hand, and went to check tighten the unions on the fuel pipelines. And did so with a smouldering cigar hanging out of his mouth.

They landed at Darwin and filled the tanks to the brim for the mammoth leap across the oceans to Japan. Dawson noticed there were no signs of lifejackets or inflatable rafts. He saw no point in telling the three other pilots Denver had recruited in Kollawonga and who were sharing the flight to Japan.

During the course of the flight, difficult though it was at times to talk above the noise of the engines, he managed to hold a conversation with them.

Bob Holmes was out from England like himself. He'd learnt to fly at Shoreham, in Sussex, under a cadet scholarship scheme. He went on to wangle his way into a crop-dusting company on the Isle of Wight where, eventually, he learnt the business of aerial spraying. When the company went out of business Bob made his way to Australia having been told on good authority his type of services were in big demand.

It was certainly true. He rarely had a day off. But after a two-year stint at the work he had a feeling that the chemical concentrates were finding their way into his lungs. He heard about Denver quite by chance and abandoned the crop-spraying job on the spot. Before, in fact, Denver had agreed to take him on.

Tim Martin, another Brit, had worked the night shift on the assembly line at Fords, in Essex, to finance his PPL and the hours to take his AFI. Then it was a matter of building his hours as an instructor to reach the necessary quota to take the commercial licence.

He too had been lured to Australia by the promise of greater things. He ended up labouring on a sheep station not far out of Kollawonga. The sight of the DC6 thundering slowly overhead, wheels and flaps down, and two of the engines trailing blue smoke, he claimed pulled so hard at his heartstrings he played truant from work and cycled after the DC6. He confessed he had got down on his hands and knees and pleaded with Denver to give him a job; he couldn't stand another day with the sheep. Denver had evidently said, "You'd probably make a better priest than a pilot. But I guess I'd better give you a chance. Now, get up boy before you wear through the knees of them, there slacks."

Nat Taylor hailed from a wealthy family who lived in North Island, New Zealand, and whose family tradition involved each member of the family, on reaching the age of 21, receiving a meagre amount of money and being kicked off into the world for three years to fend for themselves.

If after the three years they could prove they had done something useful with their life they could inherit a fair sum of money from a trust fund.

Tim made his way to Australia where he washed dishes, and waited on tables in restaurants. He also laboured for a time in a factory that made pots and pans. And learnt to fly by accident and sheer necessity!

What people knew about Jeb Carson was a bit stunted, a bit vague. There was talk of him having gone to Britain and being taught to fly by the Royal Flying Corps. He returned to Australia after the war and pottered about in flying with his name coming into prominence in the second world war when he did a lot of ferrying work. He never bothered to get a civil flying licence. After the war he worked and mixed with a variety of dubious individuals. The police and aviation authorities knew him but regarded him as a harmless, likeable rogue who kept them fully informed about the real criminals in the country.

Jeb actually died in the air. Simply dozed off into oblivion – a fitting end, many said, for the ageing man of the air.

For the unsuspecting Nat Taylor who was supposed to be enjoying his first flight, a treat from Jeb, it turned into something of a nightmare. He only twigged something was not quite right when they'd been flying a straight course for nearly an hour, and Jeb had told him they were going up for twenty minutes to blow the cobwebs out as it were. Nat looked across at him. He was sat, arms folded, his head resting on his left shoulder, eyes closed and a peaceful smile written across his face. Nat nudged him; "Don't you think it's time we headed home."

When Jeb did not respond he nudged him harder. To which Jeb, in his comatose state, tipped toward him. He summoned enough courage to push him back and much to his relief he stayed there smiling out at the world with closed eyes.

Nat claimed it was by the grace of God, and the forgiving nature of the Fairchild Argus, that helped him get it down in one piece. He couldn't even remember how he did it.

For some odd reason friends of Jeb thought he had demonstrated a bloody fine display of airmanship and paid for him to train for the private pilots' licence.

Back home in New Zealand, after the three-year absence, the family felt the incident with Jeb warranted the award from the trust fund, and he went immediately and used the money to train for his commercial licence.

He met a bad patch after that. The flying scene, the world over, it seemed was in the doldrums. He made his way to Australia and was working in the Drydust hotel, as a barman, when Denver came into his life and gave it what Nat described as a welcome change of direction.

The old, neglected DC6 plodded on gamely in the bellowing orchestra of her four big radial engines, taking them over the Banda Sea – the Molucca islands – the scattering of the Philippines – across the tropic of cancer – the Ryukyu islands.

Denver came to them from time to time with flasks of coffee and a stale sandwich and sent them up front in turn to have a spell at the controls with Captain Wun Hun Lo, a senior pilot in Oriental Air Freight.

"And before any of you guys start calling him, One Hung Low, forget it." Denver warned them. "He gets real fussed up about it. A few months ago in a bar in Japan he nearly killed an air force captain who kept on tagging him. So be warned."

Dawson was in the right hand seat when he spotted lights on the horizon. And, later, Nat, Tim and Bob crowded onto the flight deck behind him to catch their first glimpse of Japan by night. The country exuded a warm and friendly greeting by the very nature of its abundant and colourful illuminations. Then Denver chased them off the flight deck and occupied the right seat in preparation for the landing. The note of the engines rose as the props were slipped into fine pitch, followed by a power reduction for the descent. The speed came back; the flaps went down, the undercarriage followed. They swung onto the final approach. The air rushing against the fuselage softened. The DC6 lurched as full flap went down. The tapering runway lights drifted up to the nose. In seconds they were over the boundary and flying onto the runway with a jolt and squeal of tyres.

Two of the engines died from fuel starvation during the landing roll, the other two got them to the hangar of Oriental Air Freight before they too suffered a similar fate. But Denver never told his new intake of pilots. He turned in his seat and shouted back through the open door of the flight deck to the cabin, "Right you guys, we've arrived – just."

They spent the first night in a hotel with its attendant luxuries of a hot bath, a wholesome meal and a bed with fresh linen and a comfortable pillow, and, if they felt the need, a hostess to share the bed. But the VIP treatment was short-lived; the following day a jeep collected them from the hotel and drove them to Nissen hut accommodation a couple of miles down the road from the airport. The hut contained eight beds, each having a bedside locker and wardrobe, and a placard naming its owner.

Bob Holmes drew their attention to some verse written on a placard attached to one of the beds.

> This bed once belonged to a guy,
> Who insisted on getting tight?
> He drank to much one evening,
> And died in the middle of the night.

"Is that so!" Tim Martin said.

"Yes," the driver of the jeep said soberly "And he killed his innocent co-pilot and two loaders in the process. He also left a widow with two young children. That's why Mr Denver hates any man who can't hold his drink."

They later learned the driver was from Nuneaton who had cracked under the pressures of the flying and was relegated, at his own request, to general ground duties. He obviously suffered bouts of humiliation from his inability to measure up to flying but he was a good lad and nothing was too much trouble for him. He ran a shuttle service between the hut and the airport, delivering and retrieving the pilots as they went up to, and came down from, flights. In between the runs he ran errands for the pilots like collecting meals and beer from a local takeaway store.

Each member of the hut paid an equal amount to a conscientious old boy called Shinduk to look after their laundry needs and the care of the hut. He spoke little and they rarely saw him. But the hut was unfailingly neat and tidy and their laundry was never behind.

They spent the first two days getting to know their fellow employees, the engineers, the freight handlers and a small office staff led by Barbara Howton who hailed from Chertsey in Surrey. Herb Kelly was cast as the operations manager, a demanding, aggressive type, by all accounts. A short and grossly overweight figure that, smoked a very large cigar which, some claimed, he was in danger of falling off the end. He wore a permanent gathering of sweat on his brow, and unashamedly proclaimed that all pilots were nothing more than aerial couriers and were grossly overpaid.

Al King was Denver's partner, a quiet calm character but who was tarnished by a ruthless streak. He told the newcomers that for their pay he expected a pound of their flesh in return and, at times, maybe three or four pounds. He also told them it was not the company's intention for them to spend the rest of their days roaming the skies in their present beat-up, old ships. He and Denver were already drawing up plans to introduce the big jets for global operations, which should start in three years time if the company continued to rake the yen in at the current rate.

The newcomers met the aircrews as they came and went at regular intervals with the busy flight schedules. On their third evening in Japan they were dismissed and given a time and a captain they were to report to the following day.

Of others sharing their accommodation they had not met Calder. He appeared in the evening a tall, gangly American chewing the proverbial gum and intent on throwing his weight around.

"Guess you kids ain't flown anything bigger than a Piper or a Cessna," he challenged them.

They all refused to be drawn.

He turned on Nat Taylor, "Okay, kid. How many hours you got?"

"About three hundred."

"How many on twins?"

"Hundred and thirty."

"That's peanuts."

During this time Dawson lay on his bed, hands behind his head, eyes closed. Calder turned on him next. "What's your name, dozy?"

When Dawson ignored him he swaggered to the bedside. "I said, what's your name, dozy?"

For ignoring him this time Calder gripped the side of the bed and tipped it over spilling Dawson onto the floor.

From similar types he had encountered in Australia Dawson chose to act rather than react. He calmly picked himself, righted the bed, and resumed his pose on it. The others closed in on Calder and wordlessly challenged him on his next move.

He stood rooted to the spot for a good two minutes. Then he suddenly broke away and strode out of the hut slamming the door behind him.

They never saw him again; he got killed in a flying calamity the following night. According to air traffic the C47 came down quite soon after take-off. There was a suggestion an engine had failed on the climb out and in the heat of the moment, Calder's drunken stupour and a very nervous co-pilot, the propeller of the good engine was feathered in error and the C47 had no choice but to head earthwards unchecked.

The new arrivals learnt soon enough that the flying was far from a 9 to 5 job, and the aircraft were never long enough on the ground to get the servicing they deserved. It was as Denver and King said, in their pep talks, they were flying in an age when large sums of money could be earned, and earned fast, particularly in the Orient where the economy was growing under a racing political umbrella. They flew in all sorts of weather and it was expected of them to sustain the company's pride in getting the freight through to its destination.

The temperaments of the captains of the flights, the new pilots were to discover, were as diverse as chalk and cheese.

"Just you fly and deliver the goods." Denver repeated when a pilot complained about the state of an aeroplane. "That's what I pay you for."

And Ketchup Doolon, so named from his deep red complexion that resembled a well known table sauce, would laugh infectiously and say, "You say fly, Mr Denver, but my arms get mighty tired of flapping each time a motor cuts."

Dawson remembered the night he was assigned to a flight to get route experience. Ketchup was in command and Jimmy Towers occupied the right-hand seat. Dawson sat behind them on the jump seat. They didn't have a flight engineer but then that wasn't unusual in Oriental Air Freight.

They got airborne after using eighty percent of the runway length and struggled to five thousand feet where they levelled off and throttled back the desperate engines to cruise power. The DC6 growled them on through the eternal darkness on the autopilot.

They'd been flying for an hour, he and Ketchup smoking a cigarette, and Jimmy sitting wordlessly in his seat, when Jimmy suddenly stirred and shouted: "We got a fire in number four!"

Ketchup reacted calmly. He looked at the engine instrument readings, and reached across the flight deck to look at the wing with the alleged offending engine.

"I don't see anything Jimmy boy." As a precaution he disengaged the autopilot.

"Look! There it is!" Jimmy pointed to a flickering light on the instrument panel."

Ketchup refused to be hurried. Perhaps he had become accustomed to instruments and indicators, which lied in the absence of regular maintenance.

Out to the right a small flicker of flame spurted from the rear of the cowling gills. It grew brighter illuminating the wing and two engines. Then it clearly illuminated their faces on the flight deck.

Jimmy squirmed in his seat. "I bloody well told you!" he shouted, close to hysteria.

The DC6 lost a little of her composure. She dropped a wing and yawed off heading, and a hunting sound in the overall beat of the engines indicated an engine had gone out of synchronisation. Ketchup took his time in identifying the ailing engine before, with the poise and positive touch of a church organist, he closed the engine down, operated the fire extinguisher to the engine and feathered the propeller. Then he wheeled and booted the rudder to get the DC6 back onto its correct heading. He applied some rudder trim to compensate for the asymmetric power caused by the loss of the engine

"Don't ever flap like that again, Jimmy boy. Piddle on it or do something. For your sake, and mine, don't panic."

Jimmy was probably too embarrassed to reply. They went on to land at Sapporo on three engines not a rare experience in Oriental Air Freight.

Hylton was exclusively in command of the Catalina amphibian that divided its time between the airport and a mooring in Osaka bay. He was a graduate from a British university with a master's degree in mechanical and electrical engineering. He'd learnt to fly with a University Air Squadron. . He dressed in a yellow knitted pullover, which he wore over a blue check shirt and in the collar of which he sported a silk scarf printed with the colours of his old university. He wore oilskin bottoms over cord trousers and tucked his feet in yachting boots. By inclination he was a loner and flew the bulk of the clandestine intruder operations for the company. Dawson thought him a decent enough fellow but after flying with him for two weeks he felt, by the end of it, he had outstayed his welcome. It wasn't what Hylton said. He just stopped communicating.

Elliot had been with the company two years and had built up a reputation for being arrogant and moody the latter of which, many claimed, alternated between ecstasy and deep depression. He was despised by many and feared by others. Dawson's first and last encounter with him was short and sweet.

They were in the process of starting the engines of a C47. The port engine came to life normally. But the starboard proved difficult. The propeller churned over to the groaning of the starter and when Dawson flicked the master switch ON the engine gave a weak hollow cough from the exhaust and lapsed into silence.

After three more attempts Elliot leapt up in his seat and swept his hands from the engine controls. "For God's sake man, pull your finger out!"

He made five attempts to start the engine and failed. In a rage for all to hear he said, "That's the trouble with you sprog pilots. Think you know it all and yet you don't know the symptoms of an over-primed engine." He went through the motions of blowing the excess fuel out of the pots by turning the engine over on the starter with dead switches and throttle fully open.

"I'm sorry." Dawson offered.

"It's no good being bloody sorry. I suggest you go back to school and learn something about engine management." He reverted back to the starting sequence for the engine.

Three attempts later the engine still refused to start. Elliot pulled the idle cut-off of the live engine and stormed off the flight deck. Dawson followed him and as they reached the bottom of the steps of the rear hatch Elliot, in full view and hearing of the ground staff, said, "As for you, Dawson, I want to get airborne as soon as the fitter has sorted it out. Don't cock it up this time."

"There won't be a next time, captain Elliot. You obviously find me incompetent. So I suggest you find yourself another co-pilot."

Herb Kelly assigned Dawson to Dan Evans a calm, methodical captain who went about his work in the air without any fuss and bother in spite of the numerous problems they encountered in the flights. He had come to Japan after flying for a succession of small air charter companies in England which ran out of money and subsequently out of business.

Dawson joined him at the time of the Formosa contract. The island was under attack of shells being lobbed over from Mainland China who claimed the island had been taken from them back some time in history, and they wanted it returned to them. Casualties from the shelling were mounting, and essential supplies were needed. Mig fighters patrolled and attacked anything that represented aid for the beleaguered island. Goverments friendly to the islanders sought means, other than military, to rescue Formosa from its predicament. Politicians were wary of getting involved in the rumblings of a global war; China had a sound ally in the USSR.

In diplomatic circles urgent messages hummed through the ether from country to country, and telephone lines burned hot. Oriental Air freight were invited to tender for contracts. Within a week of Denver and King signing the contracts the airlift began.

Evans coaxed the struggling DC6 into the air with barely fifty feet to spare as they passed over the airport boundary.

"Gear up!" he called.

Dawson responded and watched the warning lights go out. Evans was hanging precariously on to the airspeed. They were over the weight limit.

"Clear the flaps!" Evans called again and made some small, hurried movements of the control wheel.

The airspeed marginally increased and they made a slow tense turn out over the city, staggering to gain height and dodging between the fingering architecture. They could clearly see figures sitting at the windows of a tower block.

They got out over the sea and Evans levelled off at two thousand feet and adjusted the revs and boost to cruising. After flying it manually for a spell they noticed the DC6 was porpoising, which meant it had been badly loaded. It was flying tail heavy.

"Nip aft and see if you can do anything about it, Greg."

Dawson discovered there was nothing he could do. The hold was jammed to the roof with crates.

He broke the news to Evans who engaged the autopilot, lit a cigarette and poured tea from a thermos flask. It was a five-hour jaunt to Formosa.

Evans explained it was no point climbing any higher because if they were intercepted by Migs their only means of escaping their wrath was getting low where the Migs would find it difficult to attack and, what was more, burn off their fuel rapidly.

They plodded on in the steady throbbing of the engines, pitching up and down in hot currents of air from time to time. Dawson munched at his sandwiches and sipped at a thermos top of tea and found his thoughts drifting back to his training days at Hamble. The hot sunny days, the cold blustery days, his first actual spin in a Chipmunk, and for a bit of fun Mr Farrell had taught him a loop and a barrel roll. He relived his first solo cross – country by day a most rewarding experience in that he got back to Hamble without getting lost. Then getting to know the twin-engine Oxford and learning to handle it on asymmetric power. He remembered his first night cross-country in it, floating across clusters of light whilst up and all around the stars slid in and out of the windscreen. He recalled there had always been something magical and romantic about night flying.

He thought of his fellow pupils and wondered where they were now. Rufus would no doubt be flying for Nigerian Airways. Ahmed had been destined for Air India and Carl had been promised a job with Lufthansa. Mike, Terry and Bonzo would be with the British Corporations.

He thought of the many nights they had all burnt the midnight oil swatting for their exams. But it had been great fun and worth every bit of effort. He looked down at the sea drifting beneath the engines and the wings and he was reminded of the trips up Hamble River with Karen. If he closed his eyes he could see her at this very moment in the back of the boat, the sun melting her summer dress and giving him an uninterrupted view of her truly beautiful, youthful nakedness.

"Formosa calling all stations! The island is under bombardment. Charlie patrols active in the area. Over."

Evans stowed his sandwiches and thermos. " When you're ready chuck the autopilot out and take her down to 500 feet."

They flew on for a few minutes before Dawson spotted objects high up, wheeling and glinting in the dazzling sunlight. They started to come down.

"Right! I have control." Evans called. "Tighten your belt and hold onto your hat." He started to yaw and roll the DC6 from side to side and continually varied the timing, so that he would present an unpredictable-moving target.

The descending glinting objects had grown into the blunt snouts of Chinese Mig fighters that were swinging around to come in from the front of the DC6. As soon as they lined up on a collision course they opened fire. Evans combined pitch with the yaw and roll, and sank lower toward the sea. They heard a stutter of cannon fire and ducked instinctively as the rounds shrieked past missing them by inches. Roll to the right, then to the left, skid to the right then to the left, pitch nose down, and pitch nose up and start again…. And amongst it all Evans started to sing:

Dance to the left, then to the right,
Kiss me quick and hold on tight,
I never met a gal as hot as you,
I'm willing to bet you'd make a lovely …

Slide to the left, then to the right,
Push hard up and grip it tight,
I've never had such fantastic luck
I'm willing to bet you'll make a delicious…

During his all round vigilance Dawson noticed the Migs coming in astern of them on the starboard side. He notified Evans who almost stood the DC6 on a wing tip. The sea looked dangerously close, possibly no more than a couple hundred feet below. He looked down the banked wing over the bellowing engines, thinking they would fall off the wing tip and plunge into the sea. He gripped the sides of his seat. Dan Evans was a masterly pilot. He reversed bank and reduced power on two of the engines. It rolled the DC6 rapidly, and the cannon fire went astray again.

The Migs made two more unsuccessful attacks and streaked away to the mainland.

Evans waited a little longer to make sure they were clear of further molestation and climbed them back to two thousand feet, where he re-engaged the auto pilot and they smoked a cigarette and drank tea in celebration of their escape.

The landing strip on the island was nothing but a dirt track carved out between an avenue of scorched trees. They came upon it half an hour later. Dawson thought it daunting and somewhat short in length for a large four-engine aeroplane. But Evans set the DC6 down with the grace and precision of a swan. And as they slowed down near the end of the makeshift runway and prepared to turn off Evans, in a voice he might have captured from a Punch and Judy show, said, "That's the way to do it!"

They were back in the air half an hour later with the hold filled to capacity. Injured victims of the shelling with arms and legs in splints and bandaged heads were sat on the bare floor facing the rear of the machine holding on, if they were capable, to a rope lashing draped down each side of the hold. They got back to Japan in darkness where ambulances were waiting to take them away.

Four aircraft of OAF flew the air bridge for a month solid, aided by two aircraft from a domestic airline, and five Hippo freighters flown in from America, disguised in civil markings and crewed by military personnel out of uniform.

By the end of the month the domestic airline had lost both aircraft, one to the cannon of a Mig fighter, the other over-ran the dirt strip on landing and disappeared in a ball of flame – courtesy of the high-octane fuel it was carrying.

Two of the Hippo freighters went down. And OAF had their share of the perils associated with such a risky operation.

On their way back from the island 6 Migs set upon Ketchup Doolon and Tim Martin. They were full of wounded civilians and therefore limited to how much they could throw the DC6 around to spoil the aim of the Migs. What was more they were flying on three engines. They had used the forth engine for take-off with the oil pressure hardly registering. But once airborne and at height they had shut it down.

The Migs gave them a hard time. Although two of them ended up in the sea chasing Ketchup whose propellers were all but kissing the water. The others gave him a severe pasting. They knocked out another engine and deprived him of half an elevator, punched a big hole in the rudder and damaged the hydraulics.

For nearly four hours, after the Migs stopped mauling the DC6, Ketchup and Tim wrestled with the controls to keep the machine in the air using every skill they had learnt from their training and experience.

They managed to get it high enough to lob it over the coast onto the airport where on impact it broke up in rather a bizarre and spectacular fashion.

As it struck ground it was if every rivet popped its hole and every nut sheared its bolt. It slithered off the runway onto the grass shedding engine cowlings and a number of hatches. The complete tail unit suddenly broke free and trailed to a halt behind the careering fuselage. The starboard wing and engines parted company next, and as the neighbouring wing started to drag the machine to the left, that too decided to abandon the fuselage.

The solitary fuselage carried on for another two hundred yards before it came to a halt. Then there was a long, long eerie silence. And as the rescue vehicles and a crowd of spectators arrived and looked on, a gap appeared at the rear of the fuselage where the tail had snapped off. The gap spread a little more and much to everyone's disbelief it ran the whole length of the spine to the nose, splitting the fuselage in half disclosing the injured passengers and the relieved and smiling Ketchup and Tim.

Nobody was killed.

The score for Evans and Dawson at the end of the month was a lost astro dome, a three feet diameter hole in a wing, and half a fin missing, all incurred on return flights when they were carrying wounded personnel and their choice of evasive action was limited.

Dick Orwell and Nat Parker had two engines knocked out by the Migs and they returned safely. On another occasion they lost the hydraulics and flew all the way home with undercarriage and flaps down.

Hylton never incurred a scratch. He insisted on making his runs at night, flying in specialist personnel, communications equipment, weapons and 50 gallon drums of fuel.

Denver, on hearing of his success rate, transferred all OAF flights to night operations for the remaining two months of the contract. No more aircraft were damaged or lost.

At the end of the contract Denver and King rewarded the flight and ground crews, who had participated, with a grand slam party to which wives and girlfriends were invited.

"Do you have any regrets at leaving the party early?" the young woman breathed heavily and pressed urgently against him in the darkness of the room.

He did not answer; he revelled in the liberal, succulent kisses of her mouth on his mouth and the delightful feel of her warm, naked body. He fondled her with gentle, caressing hands, preparing her, positioning her, and coaxing her into the final act of submission. She stirred beneath him, arching her back and parting her legs.

"Don't keep me in suspense any longer, Greg." she whispered urgently.

He barely caught her words; his mind had flown across the oceans to the other side off the world. It was a hot summer's day and he was sat in a small boat looking at a young woman with golden hair and whose dress dissolved in the glare and heat of the sunlight. And he was quickened in his passion and lusting by the view of her perfect nakedness.

FIVE

The pace of the flying rarely slackened and affected the hardiest of the flight crews. Evans and his wife went home to England for a hard-earned rest. Hylton chose to dodge off to Sapporo for a skiing holiday. Denison and family simply disappeared. Ketchup took his Japanese wife, Ohio, off for a tour of Europe. Dick Orwell, on the verge of another mental breakdown, voluntarily entered an institution for such people. Evidently he regarded the treatment he received as his idea of a holiday. Others said he had a crush on the big, buxom matron who treated him for some of his more personal needs. Whatever, he always returned to flying like a new man. Elliot had been booted out; nobody would fly with him, including the freight handlers.

Denver, King and Kelly transferred co-pilots to the left-hand seat and paired them with a recent intake of pilots. All of which were short on commercial experience and, within a short time, confused by the pace and mode of the flying which ran contrary to all they had been taught at their respective flying club or school.

Winter came down with a vengeance that year, heavy snowfalls, lots of icing and frequent bouts of fog. Even Tokyo had a long spell of snow when it normally only had three or four days. The long hours they spent in the air robbed many of them from knowing what time, or day of the week, it was. Take-off and landings on instruments and navigating blind became standard practise in poorly heated aircraft with unreliable radios.

They never have a chance to enjoy their living quarters. Shinduk dutifully had hot water and towels for them to shave and wash when they came in dog-tired from a flight. Other than that they only had vague recollections of short periods of oblivion beneath the blankets before an alarm clock, or Shinduk, summoned them back to duty once again.

Michael, the driver, takes them to the airport in the jeep. They trudge into operations, drugged with sleep, and receive coffee and Benzedrine tablets from a girl. A bleary scan of the met report, and the load sheet, they overhear other crews complaining to the chief engineer about the filthy state of the aircraft. Kelly moans about tired and lazy pilots who are always beefing about the iceboxes they fly. And ice, as they all know, is everywhere crunching in the control circuits and is as irritating as gritty sugar beneath the sole of a boot. They board the aircraft numbed by cold and fatigue until the engines burst into life shattering their lethargy a little. A shudder consumes the entire machine from nose to tail. The array of faces before them on the instrument panel twitch and wobble. Co-pilots read off checklists and captains confirm and double-check each item. It takes an age for the engine oil temperature to get up and before they can do the power and magneto checks.

At long last the runway stretches and tapers out before the nose. Ploughed of snow minutes previously the snow is swirling back. The controller, warm and snug in the domain of the control tower, cheerily gives them take-off clearance. Throttle up to 75 percent power, release the brakes and they trundle forward, gathering speed slowly in the bellowing rage of the Pratt and Whitney engines.

"40 knots." Connington called. "50...60...70...80"

Dawson has unstuck the nose wheel and gives a further pull on the control specs. She is overloaded and not quite ready to get on the wing. The end of the runway is bearing down on them at speed.

"90" Connington called and cringed in his seat. "100" his voice trailed off in resignation of a disaster.

Dawson gave a positive pull on the wheel and as the machine scrambled into the air he slackened the pull. The DC6 wallowed nervously and for some terse moments threatened to slam back to earth. But he continued to coax her with the controls and very slowly she began to climb. They dodged between the architecture and out over the suburbs. A shadow came down and consumed them shutting out all visual references. Tired minds and eyes revert to the flight instruments for orientation. No longer is there a feel of piloting a large heavy aeroplane, and neither does it resemble flight. It's a confinement: an aerial submarine that is claustrophobic and has a clammy shell. The instrument faces stares at them, red-eyed, wan. The noise of the engines is reduced to a muffled pulse. The hull is thumped from time to time; they know it to be ice being dislodged by the wing leading edge deicer boots and thrown rearwards where some chunks hit the tailplane. A hunting sound interrupts the pulse of the engines. Connington reached over and adjusted one of the propeller pitch levers. Harmony of sound is restored.

After flying in cloud for twenty long minutes they break out on top into bright sunshine and a crisp blue sky. Below and before them the virgin white counterpane of cloud stretches endlessly to the horizon. Dawson levelled the DC6 and trimmed it for straight and level flight after adjusting the boost and revs. He could have engaged the autopilot but he decided that Connington needs the practise. He nodded to him to take over, and treated himself to a thermos top of coffee and a cigarette. The scenery through the windscreen promotes a sense of purity and peace. He fights to stop himself lapsing into sleep he desperately needs.

Presently he moved aft to inspect the cargo in the hold. It has been loaded in a hurry in a haphazard fashion. But he is more concerned that it is lashed down securely. They said Gus Hamilton and his co-pilot died when their load slipped forward during their final approach. The aircraft exceeded its forward centre of gravity limit, and ploughed into the ground without a chance of reaching the runway.

He rejoined Connington and sat for a time looking out on the port wing and its two engines. Against the pure whiteness of the cloud the wing is a dirty grey in colour and the two trembling radial engine cowlings are dented and scratched and are further scarred by small black rivulets of oil.

Suddenly memories of the winter snow they'd left behind on the ground had his thoughts dwelling on England. He smiled to himself. He thought of the evening he'd left the solicitors office and walked home to Mrs Garret, in the deep snow. And that evening – that momentous evening – had been a turning point in his life – the letter from the bank with the funds, provided by persons unknown, to finance his flying training. He wished, earnestly, he knew who "that" person was.

He told Connington to engage the autopilot and have some coffee. They flew on above the endless layer of cloud, which is marked, with a static shadow of the DC6. They are only conscious of the passage of time when they refer to figures on the flight plan or they look at their wristwatches.

The figures tell them when to abandon the exaltation of the heights and start the letdown. They submerge into the murky depths of cloud and are plunged into a black box lit by the luminous scatter of the instrument faces, and the soft red glow of the panel lighting. An unseen voice reaches up for them from the ground assisting them with bearings as part of the letdown procedure. The pulse quickens. There is a greater need to concentrate in order to relate height, speed and heading to time. A hint of sweat gathers on the brow. A tongue attempts to moisten a dry mouth.

They descended below decision height and, according to the let-down sheet, they should cancel the approach and climb back up and have another stab at the letdown in the hope the cloud base would improve in the meantime. Dawson's recollections of the met forecast decide it is not likely to improve. If anything he reckons it will get worse. They are committed to the landing.

"400 feet... 300" Connington called anxiously. Like most pilots at this stage in his career he is dyed with the green colour of his training. He is treading a tightrope, unfairly perhaps, in the hands of another pilot. But like all newcomers to Oriental Air Freight he must sample the experience, taste the danger and learn to rationalise his fear and maintain his dignity. In not many months hence he could well be subjecting his co-pilot to a similar ordeal.

"100 feet." he shouted. Snow has packed against the windscreen rendering the wipers useless.

Dawson pressed his face against a side vision panel that spared him from being totally blind. A runway light! Or was it? Yes, there's another. He drew the throttles back and they slammed onto the runway without bouncing and without shearing the undercarriage.

The turn around is a race against the clock; the airport authorities announce they will close the airport within the hour on account of the atrocious weather.

"Yoo weerlize at own diskretion." Mr Wonsan, the airport superintendent, shouted up to them as they clambered into the crew hatch on completion of the loading. He meant that if they broke their necks on take-off he wouldn't be responsible. All the way down the route they were advised of other airports suspending operations in the tightening grip of the ice and snow until Osaka is the only one operating possibly because Denver and King insisted it be kept open. The radio is crammed with diverted aircraft calling for priority landing clearances.

The ground controllers have three stacks in operation with aircraft race tracking in tiers and waiting to be called down. Landing lanes have been set up on each side of the operating runway in an attempt to expedite the number of landings. From the frantic calls and responses on the radio it all sounds very chaotic. An aircraft has come to grief on touch down. Another has ended up in the bay. Three are demanding landing clearance now! They claim they are on their last drops of fuel.

Dawson flew the racetrack with two engines throttled back to conserve fuel. The deadline given by Mr Wonsan had prevented him from refuelling at Sapporo. He will need to demand clearance if he doesn't start the letdown in ten minutes. He grinned. Dan Evans once remarked, when they were in a similar situation, that they were sweating in the honour of the company, rationalising in the name of good airmanship and, most certainly, fighting for their survival.

Two aircraft decide to abort their approaches and the controllers grow edgy, and caustic in their comments.

"Air Freight niner two. You are cleared to 1500 feet. Report outer marker inbound. No balls-up please."

They broke through the base of the cloud with Connington calling the height and speed. It is still snowing and the wipers can barely cope. Dawson leaned toward the windscreen; he should have seen the lead-in lights by now.

"Air Freight niner two you are cleared for the right hand lane when you have visual contact."

He never acknowledged; there wasn't time. He never saw the lead-in lights from start to finish. He happened to see the runway lights out the corner of an eye, and flung the DC6 around to line up with the right-hand lane. He added power to check the descent, and slapped on full flap. They flew into the ground with a positive thump and gratefully stayed in one piece. Dan Evans had said on one occasion that a good landing was one that you walked away from. Dawson thought that he and Connington had walked away from two that day.

When they walked into the company building they were greeted by a bedlam of sound and activity. Bodies were milling around all over the place. Some smartly attired in uniform of the national carrier, state airlines or independent charters, mixed with the mercenaries of Oriental Air Freight dressed in leather fleece-lined jackets, fur-lined boots and flying helmets draped around their necks. Cigarette smoke hung like a cloud against the enamel shaded lights. The building was a babble of conversation and pockets of laughter. The over crowding had been caused by the great numbers of diverted aircraft and when they ran out of space at the airport cafeteria OAF was asked to accommodate some of the stranded crews. Telephones never stopped ringing. Kelly could be heard arguing with two pilots, one of which claimed he was going off duty, but Kelly insisted he stay in case the weather suddenly improved for him to get airborne. The other pilot really took Kelly to task and told him the aircraft allocated to him is totally unsafe to fly.

After giving money to Connington for refreshments Dawson found an unoccupied table and chairs at a relatively quiet spot on the fringes of the crowd. He felt tired, hot, and sweaty and had bit of a headache.

He had dozed off by the time Connington got back with a giant frankfurter in a roll smeared with mustard and a mug of hot sweet tea.

Connington studied him seriously for a time before he said, "Are you ready for something of a shock."

"Nothing could shock me today. I'm too tired."

Connington said: "I popped my head into operations a moment ago and they say one of our kites went down near Kobe this morning. Parker and Davies got the chop."

Dawson could not believe what he was hearing at first. Nat Parker, dead? No it couldn't be.

"Are you sure about this?"

Connington nodded. "The girls are all in tears. And I have never seen Kelly, King or Denver look so upset."

Dawson sank back in the chair, legs outstretched, his hands wrapped tight around the mug of tea.

Nat had not been his usual cheery, enthusiastic self for several weeks. But then none of them had. A greater responsibility went with the occupancy of the left-hand seat where the flying was concerned. They were all stretching themselves to the limit, flying excessive hours in ill-maintained, overloaded aircraft and often in appalling weather conditions. The occupational hazards were always there: the buffeting flights over the mountainous terrain: an aeroplane that conquers gravity on four engines but succumbs to it on three. Hills and ridges that lurk unseen in a plain of cloud or behind a curtain of fog. And then there was the rain with its regular downpours. It wasn't just local; it rained everywhere in Japan. Worn maps, outdated maps: aeroplanes, aged prematurely by neglect and abuse, fight like the faithful horse to the very last unable to avoid shedding a wing or tailplane in sheer desperation of the strain.

It was anyone's guess as to which of these perils, if any, had claimed Nat's life. Evidently he gave no warning of pending trouble. He had taken to the air that morning amongst the many other air movements. And from the wreckage located by SAR he'd flown for about an hour and a half before smashing into the side of a mountain. Perhaps there was some consolation from the fact that he never knew what hit him, or his co-pilot, Davies, a young lad from Swansea who had barely 30 hours commercial flying on his logbook.

Compassionate as they might have been Denver and King, did not let anyone dwell upon the tragedy. The show must go on. The freight must get through.

They stood Dawson down for three days and gave him the job of rounding up Nat's personal effects and sending them home to New Zealand.

He was alone in the hut when he cleared the small bedside locker and wardrobe and packed them into a grip and a battered suitcase until that all remained was a collection of letters and photographs. He sat for a time thinking of times past when they sat around the stove on a winter's night swapping their experiences of the flying or discussed news from home. They often used neighbouring wash basins in the room at the end of the hut and, whilst they shaved, they chatted about a past flight or speculated on one that lay ahead.

He looked at the pile of photographs and letters, undecided as to what he should do with them. They were probably personal and only of value to the correspondents and sending them back to a wife, mother or girlfriend would only add to the sorrow and grief of his death.

What made him do it he didn't know? He took an envelope off the top of the pile, took out the letter and began to read. At first he felt guilty of prying into something that was none of his business. Then he became curious and intrigued as a drama, which had its origins some six thousand miles away, swept up to him from the lines of handwriting:

Dear Nat,

I'm glad you received the last batch of letters and that you are well. It appears you scarcely spend time on the ground. But then I know how much you like flying.

Sorry, but I rather you did not send me any more presents. In fact, Nat, I think it will be better if we don't write to one another any more.

This is not a spur of the moment decision. I've given it a lot of thought and feel it will be better all round. I've been hoping that you'd get so tied up in the flying business, and then I would not have to write this.

There doesn't really seem any point in continuing the friendship as we once knew it, as you know as well as I do that it can never come to anything now. And even if things were different I think our true feelings have grown too far apart to mean anything.

Your life is bound up in the world of aviation and mine is firmly planted here on the ground in New Zealand.

Please forgive me, Nat, I'm terribly sorry to hurt you like this. I'd give the world not to.

I know it's not much consolation but I do so hope you achieve all of your ambitions connected with flying. And probably in years to come you will discover how silly we were. And what we ever saw in one another.

REGALE

Dawson coughed to clear a lump in his throat as he refolded the letter and replaced it in the envelope. As far as he was concerned the letter formed another element in the equation relating to the cause of Nat's and Davies's demise, and might easily sway the air accident investigation board to apportion blame.

He opened the top of the stove and fed the letter to the red-hot furnace, followed by all her letters. He paused for a moment to look through a number of photographs. A smiling girl on horseback looked out from one. Another showed Nat standing by the propeller of a DC3. A further picture portrayed the four of them holding pints of grog celebrating their first Christmas in Japan.

He disposed of all of the snaps of Regale in the stove; those of Nat he put in a wallet. He intended to include them with a letter of condolence to Nat's parents. The stove shook and the hut trembled under the pounding beat of a passing flight followed shortly by another – and another. The wind had changed. The tower was working a different runway. He closed the stove lid, secured the latches and zip on the battered suitcase and grip, and carried them with heavy steps to the mailing office at the airport.

Six

"Osaka – Air Freight niner eight. Returning to apron with suspect motor. Please notify OAF technical."

"Roger, niner eight. Take first exit right."

"Wilco. Niner Eight."

The American air traffic controller turned to his Japanese assistant, Hukoo "It beats me why anyone flies that heap of crap. It spends more time in surgery than it does in the air." He was one of a number of controllers kept on after the Korean war, to keep a discreet eye on things; the United States were determined to sustain a presence in the Far east for both strategic and economic reasons.

Hukoo said, "That airplane not fly. It hop like chicken."

"You can say that again," the controller said lifting a telephone receiver and dialling a couple of digits. He waited for the connection and said, "This is the tower. You got niner eight taxiing back in with a guffed-up engine. And in case you're interested it never got airborne. Okay."

Through the speakers in the tower a flight called for take-off clearance. The controller reverted to a microphone in his other hand. "Roger, Nippon three six. You're clear to roll. Wind zero three zero, steady at ten knots."

Another called for taxi clearance. Hukoo cleared it. Presently out to the right they heard the clamour of engines and just managed to see the dim shape of Nippon three six rising above the runway with small blue flames spluttering from the engine exhaust ports.

Out of sight on the other side of the airport an operator worked alone in a caravan working the homer service. He assisted incoming flights with bearings and headings to steer and got them into the holding pattern to wait their turn in the letdown procedure. It was all a bit hit and miss but it worked.

The controller gave permission for a Pacific Airway flight to line up and hold. His assistant gave a Tasman Airways flight permission to land. They worked on steadily, subject to the odd bout of consternation caused, as it was, by misjudgment on their behalf or an inaccurate position report by a pilot.

A Constellation had started its take-off roll as directed by the controller when Hukoo realised that he had a DC3 a quarter mile from the threshold. He had visions of the DC3 colliding with the Constellation.

The American alerted the captain of the Constellation, "Give it all you got, buddy boy. You got a DC3 sniffing your tail."

A laconic Australian voice acknowledged. And if the captain of the DC3 saw how close he was he never mentioned it. The crisis passed.

Down to the left of the control tower in the light of the hangar spot lights they could see engineers working feverishly on the naked engine of Air Freight niner eight hastened, from time to time, by the impatient Kelly. Any delayed flight caused hell in his operations schedule; Denver and King took on any work whether they could cope with it or not. They transported a vast range of commodities, from condoms to livestock, from sanitary towels to weapons, from mail to typewriters, from tourists to government agents, from ship's spares to perishable goods. Kelly had a love hate relationship with the pilots and engineers. They were qualified to do a job but rarely lived up to it. A good engineer, in his opinion, could think of good effective repairs. A pilot, worth his salt, knew how to nurse a sick ship not only in emergency but also by the dictates of the business. He switched the light off in his office, put his feet up on the desk, drew heavily on a cigar and blew a large cloud of smoke that expressed his frustration. He could see through a window and note if the engineers slackened. A persistent headache made him deposit the cigar in an ashtray. He closed his eyes and that's when the fatigued seized him. He collapsed into sleep.

He never heard flight niner zero come in. The cargo doors swung open and three trucks backed up in turn to off load the DC6. A refuelling tanker moved into position. Engineers hurried around it making a hurried inspection; it was due back in the air within twenty-five minutes.

"Any snags?" Ralph Dumper asked Dawson who had brought the flight in. Dumper had the long haul to Canton in front of him.

"Oil pressure is down on number four. And the DI is wandering. I've told technical. They're changing the filter in the DI. They're going to top the oil up on number four and put a couple of cans on board so that you can fill up again at Canton."

"What does the engine sound like?"

"Runs smoothly enough but lacks punch, if you know what I mean. I suspect a couple of pots have broken rings."

"Thanks. What's the weather doing."

"From the static in the headphones I think some storms are lingering nearby."

"Strong winds?

"I picked them up in the last hour.

"I thought as much. The isobars are really up tight on the met chart."

They parted company, Dawson wishing him happy landings. Dumper went off with Catchpole his co-pilot to pre-flight the DC6. Dawson told Connington he was free to leave. Then he organised a tray of coffee and sandwiches from the canteen and took it to the top deck in the control tower.

"Hi there." Dwight Hurston greeted him as he appeared through the trap door. "It's good to know that not everybody treats us as if we've got the plague."

Hukoo made a slight bow. "Good evening, captain Dawson."

Dawson acknowledged and invited him and Dwight to take their pick from the tray. And when Dwight told him about flight niner eight he went outside to the balcony and looked down to see the engineers replacing the cowlings of the troublesome engine. There wasn't a single pilot in OAF who didn't have serious misgivings about the Wokingham.

Its rotund fuselage and two enormous radial engines mounted on wings, more fitting for a glider, had earned it the name of "The Tub" in some quarters. In the air it was an awkward and ungainly brute to fly. It was sluggish and couldn't hold height on one engine and generally made every pilot's life a misery. Hence it was often referred to as "The Pig"

Dawson went back inside the tower. "Who filed the flight plan?"

"Your buddy, Martin."

The continuous low humming sound of the speakers was broken by an aircraft request for taxy clearance. Hukoo acknowledged. And cleared another for final approach. Dwight, keeping a close eye on the movements board, said, "The sooner one of you guys puts that ship beyond use the sooner people will be able to sleep more easily at night. I guess old Hukoo, over there, would agree to that. Wouldn't you?"

Hukoo said: "Wokingham only good as chicken hopper."

A welter of calls quickly suppressed the bout of laughter that followed his remark.

Dawson sat behind them, watching, listening, and thinking. He badly wanted to get back to the hut and get his head down for a few hours; a sense of loyalty and comradeship toward Tim made him stay on. They had always been close, coming as they did at the same time into commercial flying and moving up to occupy the left-hand seat where the critical decisions were made and control was absolute and final. But it was Nat's death that had made the bond between them stronger.

Amongst the exchanges between the tower and the aircraft the Wokingham called for taxy clearance and Dawson moved to watch it trundle from the apron and disappear amongst the gloom of the taxiways. Dwight waved a hand over his head and gave a muted cry of congratulations.

Presently it called for take-off clearance.

"Roger, Air Freight, niner eight. You are clear for immediate take-off. Wind, tree zero, gusting twenty to twenty five knots."

Dawson could picture the scene on the flight deck: Tim swinging the Wokingham onto the runway with a combination of rudder and engine. Lining up and rolling forward to straighten the tail wheel. Then nodding to Dexter his co-pilot as he opens up to full power.

The acceleration of the aeroplane is quite disproportionate to the racing, brutish sound of the two engines. It waddles along the runway, improving on its pace a little when the tail comes up. It consumes endless yards of runway reluctant, as always, to defy the laws of gravity. It has to be yanked off the ground into the air. Dawson watched its navigation lights struggling into the night sky.

Hukoo said: "Come little chicken. Now you fly."

Tim confirmed they were airborne and he was told to change to another frequency. Dwight raised his mug of coffee as a toast to the success of the flight.

Dawson was on the point of leaving the controllers when the homer operator came on the air, "Hey Dwight, niner eight is on the way back on one engine."

"Okay. Get him on my frequency as soon as he has finished with you."

By telephone, the controller brought the emergency services to alert status from standby. He also notified the fire and hospital services in the city; the local population was always expressing fears of a disaster due to the proximity of the airport.

"MAYDAY! MAYDAY! MAYDAY! Osaka – niner eight. Starboard engine failed. Unable to maintain height. Heading one two zero. Request straight in approach for two zero."

"Roger niner eight you have priority clearance for two zero. Caution: you have crosswind twenty – twenty five knots. Emergency services are in position.

Switch your landing lights on for identification. Call me when you have the field in sight. What is your present rate of descent?"

Tim's calm voice came over the air, "Unable to keep rate of descent below 700 feet a minute. Landing lights are on. Crosswind copied. Runway lights in sight."

Dwight made a general call cancelling all departing flights, and got the homer operator to start stacking the arrivals.

The shrill ring of a telephone added to the tension. Won Ling, airport manager wanted to know the nature of the emergency. Dwight had no sooner explained to him and replaced the receiver when Kelly came on the line demanding to know what was going on.

Dwight released a measure of his strain by saying, "That heap of crap of yours, niner eight, is falling out of the sky. Now, get off the line and get prepared to scrape up the pieces."

"Osaka – niner eight, we're down to 1800 feet. Can you light two zero."

Hukoo slid down through the hatch to the deck below and at the touch of a switch two parallel beads of light glowed on two zero runway.

Dawson felt concerned; he'd noted humbleness creeping into Tim's voice, a quiet strained plea. He stirred uneasily when he spotted the lights of the Wokingham piercing the darkness low on the horizon. It was very doubtful if Tim would make it to the runway. And by Dwight's and Hukoo's grave expressions he thought they knew that too. The situation both frustrated and angered him. He felt like a lifeguard who was thwarted at every attempt to rescue his drowning victim, completely powerless to reach out with a helping hand or offer a vestige of hope. He wanted to say something to Tim…

"Osaka – niner eight. I can't hold it. We're going down. I…" the voice stopped abruptly.

For a short space of time there was total silence in the tower. Dwight stood staring into space. Hukoo fidgeted nervously with his microphone. Dawson slumped on the chair; he felt the inevitable rising surge of the earth, massive, overwhelming, total and absolute in its final onslaught.

"What's happened?" the homer operator broke the silence on the radio.

Dwight said, "He's mushed it. He's down in the city." He shook himself and studied the movement tags on a glass-topped surface before him.

"I guess we'd better get the ball rolling again, Harry. How many you got in the stack?"

"Twenty three."

"Okay, start getting them down, and tell them to keep it tight. We got time to make up." He turned to Hukoo. "Get the departures in a queue at the hold."

The airport operations slowly gained momentum and within a couple of hours were back in full swing.

The Wokingham and its two-man crew lay blackened and charred beneath a covering of foam in the harsh lighting of the emergency services. Denver and King were in earnest conversation with the city fire and police department. It was a relief to them all that the Wokingham had come down in the open spaces of parkland. A number of trees were felled by the crashing machine as were some shrubs, and a number of flowerbeds were destroyed. But none of the local inhabitants or buildings suffered a scratch.

"If you ever get in a similar situation," Dawson told Connington the following day. " Head for the sea or open country and dump your load. You might stand a chance of getting away with it."

Connington was not impressed. He said sarcastically, "Pity somebody didn't tell your friend that last night."

Dawson said: "In the flying game you are learning all the time."

Karen was grooming a horse when he arrived and she looked deliciously appealing in French jodhpurs which hugged her narrow waist and clearly defined her delightful, curving thighs and long, shapely legs that from the knee downward were dressed in soft, tan coloured, leather boots.

A girl quietly alerted her of his presence. Karen turned – paused for a moment in disbelief – then threw her arms out and hurried to embrace him. She forged herself to him and clamped her lips on his in full view of the stable girls and much to the amusement of a hack setting out.

"Why didn't you let me know you were coming, my darling." she said breathlessly.

"I only had a matter of hours to pack my bags and get on a flight. It's important I see your father; we don't have a lot of time."

"He and mother left on one of his diplomatic jaunts two days ago. They're probably on the other side of the world by now." She hugged him excitedly again. "Don't look so worried, Greg. We don't need father's permission now that I am past the age of consent. We can marry in the local registry office and have James, the butler, as a witness."

She sent him to the car whilst she went and handed the reins of the stables over to a deputy she employed. He sat enjoying the peace and the silence that was far removed from the constant bustle and noise of his flying work out in the Far

East. This was England in summertime, a dazzling blue sky, the distant lofty warbling song of a lark, stables surrounding a cobbled yard, the heat drawing up and distributing vapours of hay, horse sweat and manure. This was the very stuff of England and exuded a welcome similar to that he had experienced the previous day when the big jet slid in over the verdant Epsom downs into Heathrow. Nowhere else in the world, in his opinion, did the grass grow so green and so luscious as it did in England.

They spent the night together at her house. Then he left Karen to make the wedding arrangements whilst he made a number of lightning visits. He met the Martin family in Essex and, at their request, told them a little of Tim's life before it ended tragically in the Wokingham. He thought they would not take kindly to being reminded of his death. But to the contrary they were very appreciative of his visit, and the photographs he gave them in which Tim looked out, youthful, smiling. A young man happy in his work never destined to grow old.

Pain and anguish for his caring mother at his premature snatching from life and who can readily recall his birth and her long labour to bring him into the world. Followed by the laughter and tears to rear him and help him realise his ambitions. Now he only existed as a photograph in pride of place on top of the sideboard in the living room.

Dawson motored down to Sussex next to hand over gift parcels to the parents and girlfriend of Bob Holmes. The parents complained that their son wrote so infrequently. Dawson assured them it was not by Bob's choice. But rather the pressure of the flying and lack of spare time imposed on him.

Sonia, Bob's girlfriend, said she was patiently waiting for Bob to pop the question. Dawson left her smiling and saying he would have a fatherly chat with Bob on the subject.

He and Karen spent their honeymoon in a chalet amongst the Swiss Alps during which they agreed he would not renew his contract with Oriental Air Freight when it ran out in a year's time. They also agreed that she would stay on in England rather than join him later in Japan because of his long working hours, and apart from that the stables were making ground and in a couple of years could sell at a decent profit.

He returned to Japan to find the pace had not slackened. A number of aircraft with different registrations had appeared on the scene. To replace those struck down by cracked wing spars, buckled airframes, split engine blocks, pulled rivets, leaking hydraulics, snapped piston rings, blown tyres and a couple of machines that all of the pilots refused to take aloft; Tim's death in the Wokingham had evidently promoted a defiance amongst the aircrews.

There were also new faces. Connington had gone. He'd told Kelly that he, Denver and King should be locked up; they were criminally responsible for killing Martin and Davies by making them fly a death trap called a Wokingham. In his letter of resignation he wrote:

...I am leaving the daily grappling and perpetual fear of flying the clapped-out aerial machinery of Oriental Air Freight, transporting excessive dubious quantities of freight to seedy destinations, to join an organisation where safety comes first, they supply a uniform, and provide well-maintained aeroplanes…

Conningtons's replacement as co-pilot to Dawson came in the form of a South African who everybody called Joburg, a young man with a taste for adventure and keen to add to his knowledge. He took a deep pride in his flying and quickly took to the geography of Japan, most of which Dawson introduced to him from the air. He never ceased to marvel at the endless mountain ranges, the rambling rivers, the sparkling lakes and waterfalls, the temples, the castles, the public shrines, the small cedar wood homes in the countryside, the terraced tea plantations, the rice paddies and the western architecture of the cities. Their flights took them over acres of barley and pink cherry blossoms and maple trees whose distinctive red leaves glowed like hot coals ejected from a live volcano.

On one occasion Dawson took him up around the summit of mount. Fujiyama beautifully majestic, as it was, in a pure white mantle of snow. To most of the populace Fuji was regarded as the sacred Kami of Japan. But aviators revered it because of its aid to aerial navigation; it could be seen for miles around when flying within Japan and often, when flying above cloud, there it would be fifty or eighty miles away its crown poking through the top of a layer of cloud.

Joburg, from his flying experience in South Africa, quickly learned that flying above the contours in Japan could not be taken for granted. Turbulent air roamed the heights, spun and accelerated, it waited to pounce on the unsuspecting airman. It also rained regularly and hills and tops of the mountain ranges were engulfed in mist or cloud and the unenlightened pilot lived with the anxiety of a peak or summit lurking unseen. Dawson told him that Japan had, in fact, five seasons consisting of; the Spring, the Rainy Season, the Summer, the Fall and the Winter.

Spring lasted from early to mid April. The rainy season was from mid June to mid July and was responsible for torrential rain and flooding and it was worthwhile to note, from a flying point of view, that Hokkaido escaped these perils of the weather. An ideal alternate on a flight plan.

The summer season normally began in mid July as the last clouds of the rainy season left the sky. The air temperature soared, the heat and humidity continued and the rice grew at a fast pace.

The fall presented itself between September and October. The rice was harvested and apples flooded the shops. In the north the first falls of snow appeared.

The winter season starts in Hokkaido, northern Honshu and to the west of the Japan Alps in the late fall.

It was well worth noting that Tokyo rarely had snow. Only a few days perhaps. And southern Kyushu remained dry and warm. Okinawa even more so.

The telegram arrived at the office of OAF during the hectic winter schedules on a dark, sombre evening when nobody felt particularly happy except perhaps May Wong who shared her secretarial duties between Denver and King. She went to reception to collect the telegram and took it back upstairs to inform Denver it was for Dawson.

"Where is he now?" he asked.

May Wong telephoned Kelly's office to be told Dawson was due back from a Philippines flight in two hours time.

Denver turned the telegram over and over in his hand feeling suspicious; his turnover in pilots had increased considerably in recent months. Was he now about to lose Dawson to the originator of the telegram?

He made all flight crews sign a contract. But it had evolved the contract was not worth the paper it was written on. He'd reminded a number who left at short notice about the contract they had signed. And they promptly told him that the contract they had signed made no mention about flying in dirty, ill-maintained aeroplanes that blatantly exceeded their all up weight limits.

It also irked him that many pilots used him to build hours so as to get a foot in the door of another airline. He preferred British pilots because they were unemotional, dedicated to flying, and, generally, more reliable. It was why he didn't want to lose Dawson.

To satisfy his curiosity, and knowing it was quite improper, he handed the telegram to May Wong, "Open it!" he commanded.

There was little that escaped May Wong's attention in the company. She had forewarned the directors and spared them from prosecution on a number of occasions when the law got on their trail. She knew of employees with domestic, girlfriend and drink problems. The sleuthing seemed to come naturally to her and she thrived on it.

She slit the small yellow envelope with excited fingers, challenging Denver with her smiling, knowing eyes. She unfolded the single page and as she read her eyes grew bigger and brighter. Then she threw her hands up uttering a screech of delight,

"It says what captain Doolon say." she giggled.

Denver frowned. "And what does captain Doolon say?" he was tired and low on humour.

"Captain Doolon he say, be fruitful and fly Oriental Air freight." she released the telegram and it floated down for Denver to read:

HEARTIEST CONGRATULATIONS STOP YOU ARE FATHER OF A SON WEIGHS 9 POUNDS 5 OUNCES STOP MOTHER AND BABY DOING WELL.

Majorie Swanson

It took Denver's mind back some twenty years or more to the birth of his son who now instructed on rotary wing aircraft in the military. He reached for a bottom drawer of his desk and took out a bottle of scotch and some glass tumblers. "Get King and Kelly up here." he instructed May Wong. "Tell 'em we got an excuse to celebrate."

Seven

It seemed to Dawson that he had only just got his head on the pillow when Michael the driver roused him and told him to report to Kelly ASAP. He moved about drowsily, dressing and getting his gear together. He felt so tired and jaded the last thing he wanted to do was take to the air. He'd flown every day for the last month, averaging some ninety hours a week. OAF, yet again, was suffering from a pilot famine. Evans, Ketchup, Denison and Farley were in the States converting to the new generation of big jets. Orwell had gone off voluntarily with the men in white coats, once again.

In the mean time he and Bob Holmes were training new co-pilots, checking out others for the upgrade to the left-hand seat, and coping with their normal welter of commercial operations. He arrived at the airport hanging on to his consciousness and mobility merely by the thought that there was only two months of his contract to run. Then he'd be going home to dear old England – to Karen – and to his son, Simon, who, as yet, he'd only seen on photographs sent from home. He went to the canteen hatch, ordered a mug of coffee and a supply of Benzedrine tablets and went through to operations where Kelly and Bob were waiting.

"I've picked you two guys." Kelly said. "Because it's a hot one. It's Korea and…"

"Political" Bob suggested.

"You bet. And it's gotta be done right. Our scalps are on the line according to the State Department and yur Foreign Office."

He turned to a map that covered a complete wall of the room and, using a ruler as a pointer, he briefed them on the two-part operation, beginning with a flight through North Korean into Chinese airspace to drop two agents by parachute. Followed by flying down to South Korea to deliver a quantity of arms and retrieve three American agents who'd been operating across the border for three months.

From the most recent met forecast he had drawn up a flight plan for them. And for their information a non-directional beacon in South Korea would simplify their navigation. Additionally he had given them the best aeroplane in the fleet, a DC3, code name, Blue Antelope. It had spent the last three days in the hangar having a decent overhaul and long range fuel tanks installed in the fuselage.

"Okay that's it," he said at last. "I'll introduce you to yur passengers so that you can have a chat over a drink and a bite to eat. Then, I guess, you'd better dust off the sparking plugs, uncork the exhaust ports and open up the taps."

He led them to a back office where May Wong had laid up a table for four. The men were served with a mixed grill, the woman with a Japanese dish. Dawson recognised the couple the moment they met. He'd taken them deep into China and dropped them by parachute about a year ago. Hylton had retrieved them, six weeks after the drop, by making a daring landing on the seaboard of China. He'd brought them back to Osaka where a stranger gave them tickets for an immediate flight to Tokyo and their subsequent debriefing by the CIA and BFO.

The British agent, tall, slim, a dependable looking sort of young man with fair hair and blue eyes, was accompanied by a young Oriental woman who wore a permanent smile and was attentive to him at all times.

"So we meet again." he greeted Dawson with an outstretched hand.

The young woman bowed courteously.

Kelly interrupted "I've picked you two of the ace pilots in the company. So yur in safe hands."

The agent said, "So I see. Captain Dawson and I have flown together on a previous occasion. To Lanchon if my memory serves me correctly."

Dawson nodded.

Kelly said, "I gotta go. I'll leave you guys to get on with it. Happy hunting."

Over the meal Bob got into conversation with the young woman whilst Dawson conversed with the agent.

"By your accent you are obviously from the old country." the agent said. "Where did you do your flying training?"

"A charming little place on the south coast. Air Service Training Ltd., at Hamble. Do you know it?"

"Know it?" the agent laughed. "It's my home village. My parents live in Satchel lane."

The ensuing conversation had them walking down memory lane. They talked merrily about the public houses, The Coronation Arms, The Old Hart, The Victory, The King and Queen, The Bugle, the latter of which attracted members of the yachting fraternity. Aviation and sailing formed the very soul of the village. Dawson spoke of his flying experiences at Hamble and the many nights he'd burnt the midnight oil studying for his examinations. He also mentioned his piano stints at the Coronation Arms and his journeys up Hamble river with Karen in a small rowing boat. At the end of the meal they went out to the aeroplane.

The trip to Kangye covered 700 miles and involved 5 hours flying time. They took to the air, gave a coded message of their destination to air traffic control, and melted in the darkness of the night. And as soon as they got to height and made a check on their position Dawson put Bob at the controls, and went aft to check on their two passengers. He found them keeping warm muffled up in kapok sleeping bags provided by Kelly. The agent said they planned to have a few hours sleep and could they be called an hour before the drop zone.

Dawson returned up front and they flew on for a further hour before they dropped down to 200 feet to fly under the North Korean radar web. From hereon they also restricted themselves to speaking only when it was necessary to prevent any pick-ups by monitoring stations. They pressed on out over the Sea of Japan.

After another hour of concentrated effort to pick their way through the night, at low altitude, pinpricks of light began to blink at them from the horizon. They came upon them a half-hour later and climbed a bit to help them negotiate the geography of the terrain. Dawson went through the procedure for the dispatch of the agents with Holmes, the height, the heading and the time that was based on dead reckoning navigation. Then he went aft and roused the two passengers with mugs of coffee from a thermos. They managed a conversation over the din of the engines for a time discussing the accuracy of the navigation which Dawson said was very good; they'd hit the coast on time and they were spot on track. The weather was proving to be reasonable and he didn't think the wind would wildly affect their parachute descents.

Blue Antelope was the only aeroplane of the fleet to boast a toilet. The agent and his accomplice used it in turn and togged up with warm clothing and got their equipment together. Ten minutes before the drop Dawson led the way to the rear hatch, attached them to the static line, connected himself to a safety line and drew the hatch open, inviting a rush of icy air.

"Have a drink on me next time you are in Hamble." the agent shouted above the noise of the engines and the air blasting through the open hatch. "And thanks for the pleasant trip."

"Glad to have you along. Happy landings."

The red warning light came on interrupting the conversation; the jump was imminent. The young woman took a step closer to the open hatch. The agent edged closer to her. Dawson stood poised.

The green light came on

"Go!" Dawson struck the woman's shoulder.

The male agent stepped into her place. "Go!" repeated Dawson.

In an instant he was alone in the dim glow of the lamps, facing a black void, gripped by an odd feeling that the two agents had never existed such was the uncanny manner in which the night had spirited them away. He closed the hatch and returned up front. They headed south on the next leg of the flight, fighting the growing cold, rationalising their concern at being over hostile territory, and Dawson, in particular, feeling tired. The simplicity of his wooden hut, its glowing hot stovetop, and his bed beckoned to him strongly. He shook himself and washed another Benzedrine tablet down with a thermos top of coffee. They passed over spasmodic groups of light which they sought to relate to strange names on a map whilst up through the windscreen the stars slipped in and out of view. The engines maintained their relentless pounding beat and thrust the DC3 smoothly through the night. Dawson smiled to himself in the darkness; the twinges of apprehension and uncertainty that he felt reminded him of his first solo cross country flights, by night, from Hamble, first in the Chipmunk and then in the Oxford. Then, as now, he experienced a nagging anxiety that he might get lost or suffer an engine failure. His thoughts went off at a tangent and he was wondering what Karen was doing at this very moment in time. Letters in Morse code interrupted his thoughts as Bob, having tuned into the frequency of the beacon, was now confirming it was the correct beacon by identifying the coded letters.

They listened for a time to make certain. To eventually agree it was the correct beacon. Bob started to home in on the beacon using the radio compass. For the first time in hours Dawson allowed himself to relax a little; they'd soon be on the ground doing the delivery of arms and collecting the American agents. All being well they would be back in Osaka in just over two hours and a day closer to the end of his contract with OAF: a day closer to going home, back to Karen and the first meeting with his son.

He diverted his thoughts to Bob and the sketchy letdown chart drawn by Kelly. They flew over the beacon by the indication of the radio compass, held a steady course for a couple of minutes then did a procedure turn. They passed back over the beacon and there in the distance was a solitary line of flickering lights. Bob hauled back on the specs to kill the speed, called for the undercart to go down, and presently called for flap. Blue Antelope seemed to come to a halt, before the nose dropped away and they fell earthwards gently and at slow speed. Bob called for more flap and wound the trimmer back a number of notches. The flickering lights rose up steadily to meet them.

For most pilots there was something very satisfying and rewarding about ending a flight with a neat and tidy landing – putting the wheels down on a pre-determined spot, at the right time, in the right attitude, at the right speed.

Bob Holmes was renowned for it in OAF as being the most consistent. He set Blue Antelope down adjacent to the first flickering light. There was not even a lurch as the wheels touched ground. All Dawson felt was a momentary pressure on his rear quarters through the cushion of his seat.

Bob taxied the DC3 toward a blinking white light and turned and braked by the dark forms of low-slung buildings. He cut the engine on the loading hatch side of the fuselage and said, "Whilst you satisfy yourself with the route home, Greg, I'll go and chivvy the American agents up, and get the freight off."

Dawson acknowledged, clambered into the left-hand seat and sat looking at a map and the planned route and height home. There were some treacherous areas of high ground on their way to the coast.

He satisfied himself how he would play it, and then it occurred to him that Bob was taking his time. He slid the side vision vent back and looked back toward the tail. But saw nothing. And neither did he see any activity near the low-slung buildings. He had a feeling that things were not what they should be.

He stopped the live engine and made his way off the flight deck and moved down through the fuselage fuel tanks and plumbing to the rear hatch and jumped to the ground. He walked cautiously towards the lighted windows of the buildings. He thought he saw figures loitering in the shadows of the windows. Then, as he paused to look behind him, he spotted three dark figures stalking him. And when he walked on and increased his pace he spotted a Chinese flag drooping at its mast. He felt a shiver traverse his spine and break out on the nape of his neck. He didn't have to be told that somewhere in their navigation he and Bob had made a fatal mistake.

He bounded for all that he was worth into the blindness of the night pursued by shouts in a foreign tongue, and a volley of rifle shots which served to hasten his urgency and desperation to escape. He crashed frantically through bushes and the undergrowth, stumbling and tripping many times and colliding heavily with a tree on two occasions. He had no idea where he was heading; he merely kept on running and running to an uncertain freedom.

He eventually broke out on the edge of a wood or so he thought. In the dim light of the stars the ground appeared to slope away into a valley in which the wind howled and struck his face with an icy knife. He pulled the hood of his kapok jacket over his head and masked his mouth and nose with a muffler. In the valley he stumbled into what appeared to be a bamboo shelter. In the light of a match flame he found it was both uninhabited and unfurnished. But for a man on the run it was a roof over his head and some protection from the biting, merciless wind.

Squatting down he lighted a cigarette and tried to piece together what he and Bob had done wrong to end up directly in the hands of the enemy. Had Kelly been misinformed? Had he given them the wrong information? Had he and Bob misinterpreted Kelly somewhere along the line? Had he and Bob overlooked something in the navigation?

He eventually decided there was very little point in holding a post-mortem because if he were to discover the cause it would do nothing to solve his present dilemma. He broke off two squares from a bar of chocolate he always carried on long flights; regularly beat his body with his arms to keep warm, and lived through the longest – the coldest – and loneliest night in his life. He forced himself to stay awake fearing he would die of hypothermia if he succumbed to sleep. He was also only too aware that he was in hostile territory without friends.

At long last day broke. He peered outside the shelter and saw scrubland rising up to the woodland on the hill and from which he was certain he had descended from in his escape. He noted the bearing of the rising sun and decided that if he travelled south he should eventually reach South Korea. Though how far that was he dreaded to contemplate.

His shelter stood in a line with five others and who had occupied them the interiors of the buildings yielded no clues. Unless, it suddenly occurred to him, they were monuments to the dead of a particular Chinese sect.

He had a cigarette and decided to get on the move. He'd barely moved from the shelter when the noise of a light aeroplane checked him. It came over the hills and sank into the valley and turned toward the shelters. For a glancing, optimistic moment he thought it had been sent to rescue him; the Americans had been known to make such daring flights to rescue military personnel.

But prudence warned him to be cautious. From the opening of a shelter he watched the single-engine, high wing monoplane make a number of inquisitive circuits over the huts and then decide to investigate further by coming to earth.

Two uniformed figures emerged from the machine, dressed in khaki shirts and trousers, brown boots to the knee, displaying a red star as a cap badge and both carrying revolvers as they began a search of the shelters.

Dawson timed it so that as they entered a shelter he dashed around the rear of it. By the time they were at one end of the line of shelters he was at the other end and only yards away from the aeroplane.

He sprinted to the machine and clambered into the cockpit working feverishly to get to know the way of things. Much relieved he got the engine started and that was when the soldiers abandoned the search and raced toward him firing their revolvers. He taxied the machine toward them menacing them with the dramatic revolutions of the propeller. They dropped their guns and turned on their heels.

Dawson turned through a half circle saw a narrow stretch of clear earth between the scrub, and opened the throttle. At what he thought to be an appropriate speed for the airplane he tried to coax it into the air. It failed to respond. Ahead of him an area strewn with boulders approached him. He tried desperately again to get into the air by pulling the stick right back; he had no other choice. The monoplane left the ground for only seconds before it slammed back onto the boulders smashing the propeller. After that everything whirled into confusion, he heard metal buckling, wood cracking and splitting, and fabric being torn to shreds. And the last he remembered was the instrument panel coming toward his face and he couldn't stop it.

Where the soldiers had failed; their land had secured his capture.

EIGHT

Two short, swarthy uniformed figures hauled him from the cell and took him through an unlit corridor to a door which was ajar and allowed a shaft of light from an adjacent room. He felt a growing hostility in the air and recalled the reports of the tortures this regime handed out to its prisoners.

One of his guards knocked the door.

"Bring prisoner in!" a singsong voice commanded.

Inside the room he was confronted by a short, arrogant soldier, sitting behind a bare table, whose insignia on his uniform suggested he was of officer rank. He nodded to the guards and they thrust Dawson down onto a chair and bound his legs and arms with rope. He thought quickly as to what questions might be put to him. And how best he could reply without involving Oriental Air Freight.

The officer viewed him with a sadistic grin that displayed over-large teeth and drew attention to the yellowish complexion of his skin.

"You tell me who you fly for." he sang. "Then we give you plenty food and rest."

"I don't fly for anyone. I fly for myself."

The officer looked at the guards, frowned in disbelief, resumed his stare at Dawson and chuckled, "Ha! Ha! Velly funny. I say again, who pay you to fly plane to North Korea?"

During the ensuing silence Dawson heard a match struck behind him, followed by the smell of cigarette smoke. The officer looked down at his clasped hands on the bare tabletop, unimpressed, and seemingly annoyed at the prisoner's reluctance to answer.

Suddenly he looked up and glared, "You not only funny, Eengleeshman. You also big liar." He stood and moved around the table to stand only inches from Dawson, carrying a short thin cane which he put under Dawson's chin and used like a spigot to lever his head up.

"I only ask who you fly for. Nothing else."

For his next delay in answering the pilot felt a harsh and intense prick of heat on the right side of his face. He rolled his head to avoid it and shouted, "It is my aeroplane. And I pay myself. Don't you understand!"

"Yes, I understand. But not believe. Now – if you not tell truth we force it from you. Now you understand. Yes?"

Dawson now knew it was only a matter time before his captors would carry out their threats. He winced as the cane almost pierced his skin.

"I gracious and give you three minutes to think again." the officer said and returned to his chair on the other side of the table.

Dawson feigned casualness as he glanced around the bare walls of the room. He spotted dried bloodstains on the floor and also noticed an enamel lampshade hanging from the ceiling by a solitary flex. It all combined to make him think the room could tell volumes of horror and terror.

"You have one minute and half." the singsong voice prompted him.

His mind raced and tumbled during his final moments of grace. Faces crossed his mind as if he was watching a film, Mr Barnes, the club manager, Mrs Clotter, Ron Garret, Mrs Garret, old Barnaby at the solicitors, Mr and Mrs Swanson, Karen. Then moments of his life in Australia rolled from the cells of his memory. He saw the faces of Nat and Tim when they met for the first time and flew to Japan. Now, both dead of course. Was it now his and Bob's destiny to join them?

"I generous and give you time to think," the officer interrupted. "What you say now?"

Tense and anticipating what must follow Dawson shouted, "I say again. I work for myself!"

The excruciating pain of the cigarette burns to his face jarred him into squirming, throwing his head back, and kicking against the binding of his legs, wrestling with the bondage of his arms. None of which spared him from the inhuman intent of his torturers.

He could not decide whether the brain alerted the body or vice versa. He tried to shout his protests at their treatment but it was if his vocal chords had been severed. His gaping mouth uttered nothing as the pain gripped his head in a giant vice grip. He smelt his own burnt flesh, which contaminated his sense of taste just moments before nature spared him from further pain by lolling him into oblivion.

It was, however, of short duration. The guards revived him by dousing him with a bucket of water. He came to feeling his head was on fire. The shock made it difficult for him to catch his breath and he started to retch. The salt from his perspiration aggravated the burns on his face.

The officer spat in his face and again levered his head up with the cane. "We not feeneesh yet. You try think again."

Dawson summoned his rapidly dwindling physical and mental reserves and sneered at the small, menacing yellow face; "Do what you like. I have nothing more to say."

They attacked him again with the smouldering cigarette ends, filling his nostrils with the unforgettable smell of burnt flesh. The pain began to make lights swim before his eyes. The officer's face advanced and retreated in total confusion. He seemed to be falling, faster and faster. Everything turned white – grey – black.

He came to in his cell to be greeted by the cries of distress of another victim echoing along the passage from the interrogation room. He clapped his hands over his ears to muffle the spine-chilling sounds. The cold came to him with a biting edge; his captors had taken way his kapok jacket, boots and gloves; winter had set in with a vengeance over North Korea. A rat startled him as it ran over his feet. His head burned as if the skin had been pulled tight over the skull and his facial wounds came sticky and extremely tender and painful to the touch.

The daylight at the bars of the only window in the cell was gradually overtaken by the darkness of the night. Sleep did not come to him. The growing intensity of the cold and his pain, and fear, took their turn at stealing it from him. At times he thought he was going mad; there were occasions when he thought his experiences were just a figment of the imagination or simply a bad, bad dream. And in time he would awaken from the nightmare in escape.

But the pain of his face and the rat's attempt to nibble at his toes made him face up to the reality of the situation. He stood and looked up through the bars of the window at a starlit sky and sent up a prayer requesting not necessarily to be saved from his captors but rather that he should have the resolve and determination to endure their inhuman practices.

For three days he was left unmolested, receiving but one meal a day consisting of a small bowl of soup whose flavour he did not recognise, and a meagre slice of stale bread. He ate it like a savage such was the scourge of his appetite.

"It's nearly five days, Hal." Denver said to Kelly. "What you gonna do?"

"What in hell can I do. I can't raise anybody in South Korea to check if they arrived there. BFO are saying they have not heard from their agent or his accomplice. And the State Department are doing their nut because I haven't brought their three agents back." He rubbed a weary hand across his brow. "And on top of that I don't have a spare plane to ship an urgent medical load to Formosa."

Denver shouted through to the other office. "Barbara! Get yur pretty bum in this office, pronto."

She came in smiling; "You wanted me, Mr Denver." She was never offended by his abrupt, coarse tone.

"Get hold of Hylton on the radio. Tell him I want him to fill the tanks of the Cat to the brim, and report to me ASAP."

He wouldn't have dared tell Hylton himself. Because Hylton would have told him in no uncertain terms to learn to speak correctly and take some lessons in social etiquette.

Barbara Howton came back through to say she'd been in contact with Hylton. He was on his way back from Canton and hadn't slept in three days. He was in no fit state for flying and when he got back he was going to bed for twenty-four hours.

"He can't do that!" Kelly protested. "I need him to do the medics supply run."

Denver ignored him and said to Barbara Howton. "Find out where Joburg is, and get him here ASAP." He looked over his shoulder and shouted toward his office, "May Wong, you are wanted!"

The charming, smiling oriental young woman came floating out of the office. "You called, lord and master?" she mocked him.

He respected her astuteness. "Get on to your glamour boy, Hylton. You can speak his language." He knew Hylton had taken her out to dine and dance two or three times, at the Air Captains' club whose membership was exclusively for pilots of captain rank. Denver paid the membership fee for all his pilots who flew in the left-hand seat even though he, King and Kelly were barred from becoming members.

"Don't tell him too much over the radio. Just say two of our flyers are missing and we need his help."

She went to the office where the radio was installed, asked Barbara Howton to leave, closed the door, and settled down to the radio in private.

Nobody ever found out what exchange took place between her and Hylton. But twelve hours later he set out for South Korea with Connington as his co-pilot and who allowed him to sleep for most of the flight. Their brief, given by Denver and King, was simple: Land in South Korea, get confirmation that Blue Antelope had not arrived and retrieve the three American agents if they were still hanging around. On the way home they were to call into Formosa with the medical supplies.

On the fourth day of his internment the guards came to Dawson's cell and stripped him naked in the freezing temperature, and led him along the passage to the interrogation room. His teeth chattered, his knees knocked against each other and his vitals ached. He tried hard not to shiver; he didn't want his captors to think he lacked courage.

The scene that confronted him in the interrogation room immediately charged him with compassion and anger. A naked woman lay strapped to a table. The pilot lunged forward in a rage. But the two guards restrained him and, as a warning, one of them fetched him a stinging blow on his rear quarters with the flat side of a sword.

"Let her go!" he appealed to the officer. "And I'll tell you everything you want to know."

"Beautiful white woman stubborn as flyer. She also tell lies and not think of her honour." the officer leered at him.

"Don't say anything," the woman cried out. "He and the guards have raped me repeatedly for the last week. I've told them the truth. I work for the American Red Cross."

The officer loosened the belt of his trousers and they fell to his ankles. He stood there, naked from the waist down, erect and poised.

Incited to lust by the developing scene the guards were momentarily distracted. Dawson struck out violently dashing one to the floor. But the duration of his strength prevented him from getting at the other guard who reacted by drawing his sword. Dawson heard it swishing through the air but he was too slow to get out of its way. It delivered a fine, searing cut from just below his right ear down across his back to the base of his spine. He slumped to the floor.

The next he knew he was back in his cell, still naked, laying on his clothes. He dressed slowly; every joint of his body felt iced up; he'd never known such stiffness. And the cut on his back – well, that was as sore as the cigarette burns on his face.

He did his toilet in a pot, in a corner, and dragged himself to the bars of the window. Never had a starlit sky looked so perfect and beautiful in its ethereal presentation…

"Sacrifice me, if you must." he murmured. "But please – PLEASE save the woman."

At first he thought he was imagining it. Then he heard it again: a forced whisper calling to him in an Australian drawl.

"Hey there, cobber. Put a hand out of the door bars and around to your left. I've got a cigarette for you."

Dawson responded slowly, cautiously.

"Hurry it up sport or the Chinks might catch us."

As Dawson groped blindly for the cigarette a door opened at the end of the passage, lighting up the entrance to the cells. In his haste to take the cigarette he knocked his hand on a bar and it spiralled from his hold and lay smouldering on the floor. And on hearing boot steps approaching the cell he swept himself into a dark corner and pretended sleep.

"You velly funny prisoner." the guard shouted through the bars of the door. "But you no laugh tomorrow. Guards powerful and strong. And not have woman for long time." the voice trailed off into a mocking chuckle. The door along the passage slammed to shutting out all light and it went very quiet.

The Australian got a burning cigarette successfully to him this time and it came as a luxury. The smoke irritated the wounds on his face. But after inhaling several times he felt more composed, more hopeful, and more confident.

He owed it to the Australian and his supply of cigarettes for getting him through the next interminable bitterly cold night.

By the time the next day dawned he was so cramped by the cold it took him several minutes to straighten up and move about to bring some sort of flow to his blood circulation.

About mid morning a guard arrived with a tray carrying a bowl of rice and bean shoots, a canister of runny sauce with lumps in it, and a metal mug containing a black liquid resembling coffee which he discovered later tasted nothing like it.

"The officer, he say you prepare for great love act today."

Dawson signalled with his eyes that he was not amused. The leering expression of the guard vanished and he retreated from the cell cautiously. Dawson devoured the food in seconds; he'd had no food the previous day and the intense cold compounded his need to find warmth. He was so hungry he was tempted to eat the wooden bowl

The Australian started up another whispered conversation with him and he learnt his name was Brett Brown, from Sydney. He was gun running when he took the wrong fork on a river and ran straight into the hands of the North Koreans.

Dawson said: "It doesn't sound as if you've been roughed up by the Chinks."

"That's simple, sport. I'm a convincing liar. You're not."

A door squeaked open at the end of the passage bringing their conversation to an immediate halt. The all-familiar boot steps approached. Dawson drew a deep breath and fought to rationalise his fear as the key turned in the lock of the cell door. They had come for him.

The woman lay naked on a bare wooden table her arms bound to the table legs at one end, and her parted legs bound to the table legs at the other end.

"Now you see how my soldiers make great lovers," the officer said.

"No! No! not again. Please!" the woman screamed. "I'm hurt. I'm bleeding."

Dawson's mind fragmented into a fit of uncontrollable rage. He lashed at the guard by his side and sent him sprawling to the floor. He sprang on to the back of the other that threatened to rape the woman and thrust his fingers in the guard's eyes. He had barely immobilised the man when the former guard dived at him. He stepped aside and his assailant crashed onto the concrete floor and Dawson seized the opportunity to kick his head until he was unconscious. Out the corner of an eye he saw the officer hurrying for his gun and holster hanging on a chair. Dawson hurtled across the room, collected the officer's desk, and steered it with the force of a battering ram. At the moment the officer stooped to collect his revolver Dawson crushed him against the wall with the table. He bellowed a protest of pain and collapsed. To which Dawson took the gun, thumbed the safety catch off, held the barrel at the little man's head and pulled the trigger. A treatment he meted out on the guards.

For a moment his thoughts raced about in confusion. Were there other soldiers likely to pounce into the room? Should he release the woman? Should he go and let the Australian out of his cell?

He eventually found cell keys on one of the guards and went down the passage. He put the bunch through the bars of the door and told Brett Brown to find the correct key whilst he attended to the woman.

He discovered the sleeping quarters of the officer next to the interrogation room. After releasing her bonds she was so weak he had to carry her to the other room. He dressed her in a skirt and top, which had been taken from her and, under her directions, he found a towel to stem her bleeding. Then he wrapped her in blankets.

In a feeble voice she told him that as far as she knew the guards and the officer were the only ones she had seen since her capture. Dawson, once again, experienced a bout of confusion; he'd thought all along that he had been taken back to the spot where he and Bob had landed Blue Antelope. The fact that he had been taken elsewhere after his failed escape in the light aeroplane explained why Bob was absent.

The Australian arrived in the room and after hasty introductions volunteered to do a recce outside to ensure they were not under immediate threat from other enemy troops. Before he went he and Dawson dumped the dead bodies in the cells and relieved them of all their weapons and ammunition. And in Brett's absence he went through the interior of the building collecting any item that would be useful to their escape. There wasn't much. Some oddments of clothing that were too small for any of them but which they would have to use during the escape. A couple of broom handles and a blanket to make a stretcher for the nurse; she was in no fit state to walk any distance. He found more guns and ammunition, maps, a compass and binoculars.

When Brett returned Dawson had got a Primus stove working and was preparing a basic meal of soup, brown bread and tea. Brett returned with a chicken, which he had plucked and drawn. He said there were several more running loose in the yard. And whilst Dawson helped the nurse to take the soup, bread and tea Brett arranged an open tin over the Primus and put the chicken in to cook.

Over the meal the two men agreed they should get away at first light next day. Brett reckoned they were about 30 miles from Nomansland that separated North and South Korea. He claimed they should head due south on the compass and, all being well, they'd be back in South Korea in four days at the latest.

Dawson did not share his optimistic prediction. But he said nothing. It was frightfully cold out there and they were poorly equipped with clothing. They would have to be constantly alert for NK patrols and possibly searching aircraft. They'd be travelling through a terrain hidden under snow. They'd be carrying the nurse on a stretcher with slippery conditions underfoot. Not to mention how they would treat her medical condition.

Whilst the woman slept peacefully that night, Brett fashioned a sturdy stretcher with two blankets and the broom handles, and Dawson, using kit bags taken from the dead troops, packed them with a meagre supply of food and their other belongings.

When dawn broke they made their departure.

NINE

In a small notebook Dawson wrote:

DAY ONE. We travelled for six gruelling hours today through a white, cold, hostile wilderness, during which we slipped into a crevasse and stumbled down a hill, which were disguised by snow. In the process we lost our grip on the stretcher. The nurse is not well.

We pitched camp before nightfall. Brett fashioned a lean-to shelter by using a canvas cover taken from the stretcher, as were the broom handles. It did little to cover our heads but it served as a break from the icy wind.

We brewed a most welcome pot of coffee on the Primus rather than light a fire that might attract attention from unwelcome company. I managed to get the nurse to take three sips of coffee. Then she fell back exhausted. Her marble face does not reassure me. Brett and I huddled up to her in an attempt to keep her warm. He reckons we have only covered a miserable 4 miles today and suggest we convert the stretcher to a crude sledge in the morning to aid our progress and to conserve our strength. He admitted his four day estimate to reach friendly territory was a little too optimistic. Seven days is a more likely figure.

DAY TWO. We made better progress today: six miles by Brett's estimate. The wind was bitterly cold and never stopped howling. Around noon we cut eye slits in our scarves and tied them around our faces, the idea being to protect our eyes against the constant glare of the snow.

After helping Brett rig the shelter before darkness came I climbed cautiously to the summit of a nearby hill and surveyed the area through binoculars. I worry constantly about a surprise encounter with an enemy patrol.

The scene that confronts me however conjures up something quite different in my mind. The white desolation resembles the surface of an unknown planet and we are its sole occupants. I am overcome with an eerie feeling that we are to be swallowed up by the creeping whiteness, which has already devoured every vestige of plant and tree life.

When we huddled up to the nurse tonight to protect and keep her warm I think I did it more out of loneliness. The only companions we have are the stars twinkling up there before us. I eventually fell asleep wishing upon a star and it's needless to say what I wished for most of all.

DAY THREE. A calamitous day. We lost our footing on a large hill and our actions started an avalanche. It took Brett and me a frenzied half-hour to find the nurse and stretcher buried beneath the snow some three hundred feet down at the base of the hill.

Surprisingly it sparked some life from her and, unlike yesterday, she actually took soup and coffee today and murmured something about me needing treatment to the festering sores on my face. I must confess they do pain me from time to time. But I try not to think about them. My priorities are to get her to safety and the urgent surgery she vitally needs to stem her loss of blood.

Braving the elements, I undressed to get at my vest. Then I delved below the blankets and substituted the blood-soaked wadding of her wounds with the folded vest; a delicate and very personal gesture that left me feeling very embarrassed. The nurse touched me with a weak hand and smiled her thanks up to me. And that made me feel a little better.

Despite the cold we are beginning to smell. I notice it when we huddle up for the night and the body odours creep from our clothing. A long, hot soak in a bath would not go amiss.

DAY FOUR. We set out in the morning with high hopes. During the day a light aeroplane pottered around to the south of us and in line with the route of our escape. It eventually flew west and turned north. We had barely relaxed and got on the move again when a jet swept low over our position. That too hung around for some time whilst we crouched in the snow desperately hoping it had not noticed us.

At last it made off. We breathed a huge sigh of relief and moved on southwards. Brett reminded me that we should be in South Korea within the next sixty hours....

The shots took us totally by surprise. We flung ourselves to the ground and shielded the nurse.

"Did you see where the shots came from?" Brett raised his head cautiously.

"No idea."

We waited.

Brett said, "I'll make a quick dash to pull 'em. You try to spot where they are."

"I'm ready when you are."

Several shots rang out as Brett ran across a patch of open ground. I spotted a number of heads bobbing up and down on a hill sloping to the right of us.

Another volley followed when he ran back to me. He checked the chamber of his revolver and told me to do likewise. I told him I'd seen three, possibly four heads.

He said, "They normally patrol in fives."

I eased the binoculars from my chest and viewed the hill. I stirred uneasily at what I saw. There were five of them all right and they were moving up the hill in our direction, which I reported to Brett

"This is what we'll do. " he said. "I'll make a run for it and you pick off as many as you can. Every bullet must count. So don't fire until they are at close range."

I grew so tense I discovered I was holding my breath.

"It could be that they think they have killed us already." Brett said in low tones. "See how they are exposing themselves."

Until my internment I had never had the desire to kill anybody. It troubled me to think that I must kill again or be killed myself. The red star on their uniform caps showed clearly as they advanced toward us, slinking, pausing and changing direction regularly in an attempt to pose as a difficult target.

Twenty-five yards separated us when Brett rose up and sprang at them, moving in a zigzag pattern, and firing from the hip. The air went wild with an exchange of shots. During the commotion I thought I heard a cry from behind me. But I was too busy; having brought one down I was sighting on another attacker. I discharged a round and my second victim threw his arms up, uttered a heavy groan and slumped into the snow. Another figure made a lunge at me. I fired at point blank range, stepped aside and he too crashed to the ground. And to make certain he could cause no further trouble I put a bullet in the side of his skull.

Suddenly I am surrounded by a suspicious silence. Nothing stirs except the relentless spiritual wailing of the wind. I'm wary of one of their number lying out there feinting death and is just waiting for me to make a false move and he'll get me between the eyes. And where is Brett?

I finally mustered the courage to take stock of the situation. I count five dead soldiers. The nurse too is dead, victim of a stray round. I thought I heard her cry out during the height of the gun battle. And the truly, courageous Brett Brown, much to my shock, has also met his end many, many miles from home.

DAY FIVE. I am glad to be on the move away from the bodies, which were strewn around me all night. I left the bodies of the soldiers where they were but put the nurse and Brett side by side, covered them in snow, and said what I thought to be an appropriate prayer. The earth is frozen and I have no tools to dig a grave. My bones feel so cold and brittle I fear they will snap if I stumble.

I trudged along all day in the desolation of the white wilderness. As night fell I used the last of the fuel for the Primus and made a mug of soup. I spent the night wrapped in a blanket and covered by the canvas sheet used on the stretcher. I feel exhausted and worry that I may become a victim of hypothermia and never regain consciousness.

DAY? For some reason or another I have lost count of the days. I am so cold and hungry that a part of me wants to sign off from the hopeless situation in which I find myself. I am so tired I could sleep indefinitely.

And yet there is another part of me, which wills me to survive by visiting me with scenes of a beautiful young oriental woman standing on a wooden, rickety bridge, looking reverently up at the majesty of mount Fujiyama. I'm certain I've seen her somewhere before. Though I can't remember where or when it was.

After ten days on the run and dangerously close to death he reached the end of the snow plain and looked down on an airstrip that was inhabited by an American Fighter Wing. They were not to know who he was and were naturally security-conscious.

He made his way down the hill to the dispersed fighter aircraft and blister huts. Suddenly a shot rang out and he grabbed at a searing pain in his left arm. He fell backwards, striking his head on the hard frozen ground. The blue sky spun in to a grey emptiness – into a solid, dark immobility.

"Will someone take that phone!" King shouted. He was talking on another phone to a company who urgently wanted a spare part for a ship stranded in Manila. Barbara Howton took it. Kelly was up at Toko Main airport getting the facilities organised for the arrival of the company's first big four engine jet transports from the Boeing company. They were due to start long haul freight services in a fortnight. Denver, Evans and Ketchup were also in Toko.

Barbara Howton was running operations. In essence May Wong was running the company and King pottered around trying to help where he could. By a stroke of luck he managed to get Hylton on the radio and arrange for him to fly the part for the ship to Manila. He couldn't do it straight away. But he reckoned he'd get to the ship within twenty-four hours. King informed the customer who shouted for joy over the telephone; evidently he had contacted eight other freight companies and the best delivery they could give him was a week.

King put the receiver down with a triumphant grin and lit a cigar.

May Wong appeared by his side. "Have you decided how we are to word the telegram to Captain Dawson's widow and the relatives of captain Holmes?" she said; he had been avoiding the issue for three days.

"Not that again." he groaned. Hylton and Joburg had made the trip to South Korea and the only information the intelligence network could give to them was that an aeroplane, from Japan, had made an incursion of North Korean territory and according to NK radio broadcasts the crew had been executed. In the absence of any other aircraft reported missing it was very likely it was the OAF plane and its crew. But King would have been happier to send the telegram if he had sure-fire evidence.

"Yes – this again." May Wong said. " You have to face up to it sooner or later."

"We don't have proof."

"In the circumstances I think we have enough. I have contacted all the civilian operators and they don't have any planes missing. And the military say that as far as they're concerned all their planes are accounted for."

"Right!" he hauled himself up from the chair, rolling the cigar around in his mouth, "We regret to inform you that your husband, captain Gregory Dawson is missing, presumed killed – stop – letter to follow. And do the same to the family of Holmes." His tired figure moved to the door. "I'll leave you to organise it, Sugar Plum. I'm off to get some shut-eye." He hadn't slept in nearly 72 hours.

"If you can wait a while," May Wong suggested. "I'll drive you to your pad and do the telegram on the way."

She hurried through to Barbara Howton in the operations office. "If you get any problems, contact me and let him sleep."

"I've got one at the moment. I haven't got a captain for the Canton flight, tomorrow; Dick Orwell has gone sick."

May Wong looked up at the wall-size movements' board. After a time she said, "I see Joburg is due in at 0800. Tell him that King has said he is to take the Canton flight in the left-hand seat. He's done the flight before and he has logged several hours on the DC6 as a co-pilot. And tell him he'll get captain's pay as from that flight." She paused. "If nothing happens in the meantime I'll relieve you at midday."

Dawson walked casually along the waterfront of Osaka Bay in the evening sunlight, inhaling the warm, fresh, salty tang of the sea. It was unusually quiet and deserted.

He could not remember when last he felt so relaxed and free. Free of pain, of anguish, of fear, of harrowing faces, menacing words, bitterly cold nights, snow, hunger and the threat of death. Life had come to be very precious to him. He found himself marvelling at, and appreciating, the beauty of the crimson disc of the sun hanging low over the Bay and the manner in which it painted the sea and sky. To the rear of him he heard the distant rumblings of activity in the port and docks. Occasionally a ship's siren echoed across the water. Some hundred yards ahead of him he noticed a canvas set upon an easel which hid the head and upper torso of the artist from view.

Down to his left he was distracted by a small boy standing on the prow of his floating home, precariously trying to keep his balance whilst emptying the contents of his bladder. Suddenly he tumbled into the sea, to be promptly rescued by a scolding parent who commenced to spank his rear quarters in punishment. The angry mother gabbled in her native tongue up to Dawson. He didn't understand a word; he grinned sympathetically down at her and walked on.

On drawing level with the canvas and easel the artist turned out to be a young oriental woman with narrow, swept eyes, high cheekbones, slightly flattened nose and a small delicate mouth. When he arrived she was in the throes of putting the finishing touches to her work – a dab here – a stroke or two there – she paused and stood back to note the effect.

The foreground of the painting depicted the huddle of sampans against the quay wall. Out in the Bay a ship lay at anchor. The expanse of the sea reached to the horizon and melted in the blue of the evening sky. Dawson rather liked it and thought he'd like to own it as a reminder of his time in Japan.

The woman turned to him smiling shyly, "You are interested in art, yes?"

He grinned back at her. "I don't profess to be an artist. But I think your painting is very good. I'd like to buy it from you."

"Me, velly solly. Many wongs on painting, you see. You must never pay fu bad painting."

"You as the artist might see the mistakes. I see nothing wrong. I truly would like to buy it from you."

She pointed at the canvas with a brush, "It is plain simple to see," she said. "The sea is gwey and sky is blue. But must show touch of setting sun, you see."

She began packing away her materials.

He said, "Regardless of what you say I would like to buy the painting from you."

She ignored him and busied herself dismantling the canvas and easel. He did not press her further. He merely offered to carry the easel for her, and she accepted.

He walked by her side, not knowing where they were heading. And he didn't greatly care. He felt safe and at ease in her company. In the gathering darkness they walked through the brightly-lit streets, occasionally stopping for her to view a shop window. Flashing neon-lighted advertisements struck at the night sky. Strains of oriental and western music rose and fell amongst the hustle and bustle of pedestrians and traffic. More than once he had to thrust her clear of a careering taxi or rickshaw.

The pandemonium faded as she led him into a side street and leant against the wall of a store shaking with laughter, "You know me think most funny those cabs and wicky boys. They mad every day."

He laughed with her. "The rickshaws are more dangerous. They could run you through with a hand shaft!"

She gave a squeal of delight, "A wicky boy velly funny last week. He take wong way in street. He t go in caff, and out at back."

"With the rickshaw?"

"Yes," she screeched. "But wheels not go in. The wicky stop, and boy cawwy on and cwash into man and lady having meal." She waved her arms aimlessly in imitation of the chaos. "Couple mad! Boy mad! Waiter mad! Evybody mad! All good food on woof, on clothes." She dropped the canvas and materials and leant against him bubbling with amusement. After his ordeal of recent months he found her warmth and gaiety pleasantly reassuring.

She went very still, looked up at him and said softly, "Me not happy like this for velly long time. You must be lucky fu me,"

`He put a hand on the side of her face and kissed her on the forehead. "I think the same goes for me," he said.

"Now we both happy, yes. Please – I show you whu I live."

They walked for about ten minutes before they came to a cedar wood dwelling set amongst a number of others in the suburbs of the town.

"When may I see you again?" he said when she relieved him of the easel.

She smiled at him in the dim light of a porch lantern, obviously pleased and grateful at his request. "I feeneesh work at six o'clock. You meet me Fwiday, yes?"

"Where do you work?"

"Oh yes, velly solly, the lamp company next to airpowt. You know it?"

"They make the lanterns of silk, and paint them by hand, don't they?"

She nodded and said, "We also make glass lamps. We do much expo work."

He held her hand, "Until Friday then."

She put a hand on top of his, "Please, you join me for cha-no-you, Friday, yes?"

He knew she was referring to the traditional tea ceremony in Japan, and in which he had never participated. He accepted and added, "By the way, I'm Greg Dawson."

Still allowing him to hold her hand she took a step backwards and bowed courteously to him "Me, Kimuko. Kimuko Kagoshi."

They made their farewells and he walked to the end of the street where he paused and noted she had waited to wave to him before he disappeared from view.

When he reached the main roads he hailed a cab to take him back to his hotel accommodation provided by Denver and King when he was discharged from hospital. He retired for the night and for the first time since returning from his perils in North Korea he was both intrigued and relieved to discover he could cope being alone in the darkness without a light. Up to today he had never ventured outside the hotel after nightfall unless he had company. And in his apartment he'd never slept at night without a bedside lamp illuminating his surroundings. The darkness had haunted him relentlessly with the inquisition and tortures of his imprisonment. He awoke sweating and writhing from the nightmares and the lifeless images of the nurse and the courageous Brett Brown.

In his apartment he made a pot of tea, and sat in his bed smoking a cigarette with the room in darkness. Through a window opposite he could see the lighted windows of the neighbouring tower blocks. He felt contented, happy and relaxed, and was aware that Japan had become very much a part of him with its architecture, its strange traditions, its enchanting culture and its polite and courteous people.

After the bullet got him in Korea and put him out, the next he remembered was the feel of fresh white linen and the sight of a bedside locker portraying a jug of water hooded by a glass tumbler. The air breathed the smell of ether. In an adjacent bed a figure slept with the bedclothes drawn high about the ears.

"Good morning, captain Dawson." a nurse appeared at his bedside. "How are you today?"

Everything at the time was somewhat vague. "Where am I?"

"An American hospital in Japan. You were flown in from Korea a week ago."

"I've been here a week!" he stirred.

"Yes. You had a wound in your arm. And you were delirious and kept on shouting out and waving your arms about." she fussed around him rearranging the bedclothes. "Would you like to sit up?"

He nodded and she helped him. And then she put a thermometer in his mouth and took his pulse.

"Was I a lot of trouble?" he said later.

"Not for long. We gave you an injection to calm you down."

"How did you find out who I am?"

"In your delirium you frequently mentioned Oriental Air Freight. So we contacted them and they rushed over here and identified you. They are very keen to talk to you as soon as you are able. They were hoping captain Holmes would be with you." She paused. "Personally, I don't think you are quite ready for visitors. I think we need a couple of days to clean you up, tidy your hair and face, and see to your diet."

He agreed, saying he was more than ready for a good soak in a bath of hot water followed by a chicken curry.

His visitors started to arrive three days later. Denver and King came first and gave all the impressions they were concerned for his health but were mainly interested to know how he and Bob had come to end up in North Korea. And why Bob wasn't with him.

He patiently spent an hour explaining to them all that had happened. They listened in silence, fidgeting and wincing at times as he recounted his harrowing interrogation and tortures, and described the circumstances in which the nurse and the courageous Brett Brown had met their death.

They left greatly relieved that he had not given anything of value to his North Korean captors. And told the nurse to take good care of him.

There followed an official from the British Foreign Office who was keen to learn anything about the male and female agents he had dispatched. Neither agent had confirmed they had arrived in China. The pilot was certain they had dropped the agents in the right place. But the official was not convinced. In his opinion if the two pilots had landed by mistake in North Korea it was conceivable they had also mistakenly chosen the wrong drop zone for the agents. Dawson suggested the agents were maintaining radio silence to avoid revealing their position to the Chinese. The official left unconvinced and grim-faced.

Next came a couple of guys from the CIA who, unlike his previous visitors, came with some interesting information. In recent months the USAF had lost an undisclosed number of aircraft. And only in recent days had intelligence got proof that insurgents from North Korea had sabotaged a navigation beacon near the northern border of South Korea. But what had been overlooked was the fact the North Koreans had erected a beacon on their territory some ten miles distant and equipped it with the same frequency and ident code. And as a result aircraft homing to the beacon were delivering themselves directly into the hands of the enemy. A clever trap indeed!

Unlike Denver, King and the visitor from the BFO, the staff from the CIA didn't interrogate him. They simply got the information out of him by rational discussion and idle chit-chat. They left him after quarter of an hour apologised for his injuries, complimented him on his courage, and asked for his permission to speak to him again at a later date if they felt it necessary

He spent the next two weeks undergoing surgery to the infected burns on his face, a painful and unpleasant process and a period he was pleased eventually to get behind him. He moved on to getting up and about with the aid of the nurses.

On being discharged from hospital he was sent on a skiing holiday to Sapporo at the company's expense. He'd never been on skis before so he was limited to the nursery slopes. The crisp air up in the heights, the exercise, and the regular meals did much to rebuild him physically and provide him with a healthy tan.

Mentally, he felt a little fragile. He was permanently conscious of the scars on his face. He could never go back to Karen like this. He could quite imagine her shock at learning he had survived when she was just beginning to recover from the telegram reporting his death. What was more he had lost all inclination to go home to England; Japan and its ways and its people had become very much a part of him. He told all this to Denver and King and insisted they put off notifying Karen of his survival. It would be too much of an upheaval for her and her family, he said. And he needed time to adjust.

Following his vacation up at Sapporo he was allocated an apartment in a hotel and he arranged with the company for him to get back to his work in the air. Dan Evans had cleared him fit to return to operations that very day which also marked his first meeting with Kimuko. The second meeting with her could not come soon enough.

Her smiling face appeared amongst the seething mass of workers as they surged through the factory gates.

"You wait long, Mista Gweg?"

"Only a couple of minutes." he took her arm and steered her to a rickshaw he had retained. He helped her in and told the runner to make haste to get clear of the heaving bodies. He smiled; Kimuko sat erect, head held high, smiling proudly as the rickshaw weaved in and out of the pedestrians and traffic, often drawing the scorn of the motorists.

Two miles on he got the runner to drop them in a main street, and they made their through the side streets on foot. As they walked she explained that she lived with her sick mother. Therefore her first duty when she arrived home would be to attend to the needs of her mother.

He sat alone on a wicker chair in a small room, and it was peacefully quiet. A round pink paper lampshade hung from the low ceiling. Each wall told a story in pictures. Stories of peasants bending their backs working the rice paddies. Of others in conical hats and carrying baskets on their backs as they tended the tea plantations. Another wall was devoted to a pagoda surrounded by birds of rich, colourful plumage. The forth wall of the room depicted mount. Fujiyama gloriously resplendent in a mantle of snow as viewed by a young oriental woman dressed in a white kimono, standing on a quaint wooden rickety bridge

He frowned heavily and his thoughts tumbled about in confusion; he had seen this scene many time throughout his life. But he could not determine exactly where or when it had been. He'd had the same experience the first time he met Kimuko. Whether it had been in a dream or during his rare excursions on the ground in Japan he did not know. But he was certain she had figured in his life before their meeting in the Bay earlier in the week.

She broke into his thoughts as she appeared, dressed in an attractive white kimono trimmed with orange brocade with her jet-black hair drawn up on the crown of her head. He'd never seen anything quite so beautiful, so poised – so elegant. Her presence brought an added peace and serenity to the room.

"My mamma now sleep. Please, Mista Gweg, you dress for cha-no-you?" she said softly and led him to an adjacent room and dressed him in a kimono and zoris.

They returned to the other room. She got him kneeling on a tatami before a long, low table. And thus began the serious, contemplative ritual of the Japanese tea ceremony.

From her he learnt a tea bowl was known as a cha-wan, a kettle as a cha-ire, a whisk for emulsifying the tea, as an acha-sen and a bamboon spoon as a cha-shaku. She explained that one's rank or status determined one's position at the table. And it was most important for all participants to behave with the utmost attentiveness.

Following a period of rest she opened up what she referred to as the goza-iri, the second meeting, by serving the whisked tea in the cha-wan. It was passed from individual to individual who took a modest fill of tea before wiping the rim with paper and passing the communal vessel on to the next person.

The ceremony concluded with the serving of usu-cha, thin tea. Following which she announced they could now dispense with the attentiveness of the occasion and engage in general conversation.

The conversation moved back for a time to the tea ceremony and she told him how the ritual brought a welcome calmness to her life after a busy day in the factory. She also confessed it also helped her cope with the care of her sick mother, which took up most of her leisure time.

From what she subsequently told him her life had not been an easy one. Her father had died in the war. Her mother had been on the fringes of the atomic bomb dropped on Horoshima. Kimuko was one of the fortunate children who, days before, had been evacuated. But in due course it fell to her to take on the responsibility of nursing her ailing mother.

He reached across and gently squeezed her shoulder. "Your life seems to revolve around little other than your work in the factory and caring for your mother. And yet you keep smiling."

She looked shyly up him, her small lips parting in a smile, her eyes slanting, "Yes. It must be so. My painting, give me gwate joy. Each month me go and stand before Fuji, my Kami, and thank him in pwayer. He bring great peace to my body and soul, and teach me to be patient in my desire to have a suitor."

As a matter of courtesy and in consideration of her having mentioned the need to start her day early to care for her mother and to get to the factory on time he did not prolong his visit. He went to the other room and got out of the kimono and zoris. At the main door of her home he took her hands in his. "Thank you for your hospitality this evening, Kimuko." he said. "It was most kind of you."

"We meet again, yes, Mista Gweg?"

"Yes, of course"

"And you teach me good English, yes?"

He sealed his agreement by kissing her on the forehead. And left.

The following week he got back to flying in earnest after renewing his year's contract with OAF in which he stipulated he would only work a five day week. King and May Wong were busy with the jet operation out of Tokyo at the time and Denver signed the contract on behalf of the company.

When Dawson wasn't flying he was with Kimuko. They set up home together after he purchased a larger and more modern dwelling that accommodated her mother in greater comfort. They lived quietly, privately, and gave the impression that their relationship was of a platonic nature. It led to a lot of speculation behind their backs.

At a weekly management meeting, a month before Dawson's contract was due to expire, May Wong said "As a matter of courtesy to his family and as a token of respect for the name of this company I think his family should be notified of his existence. Before, in fact, we allow him to renew his contract next year."

Denver and Barbara Howton nodded. King said, "Don't look at me! It was you who pressed me to send the telegram, Sugar Plum. And the covering letter in which I said he perished in the Sea of Japan and was probably eaten by sharks when his wife said she wanted his body flown back to England. That too was your idea, Sugar Plum."

Denver said, " I guess we ought to find out if he intends to stay on in Japan and, if so, what are his plans. How do we know he hasn't been in touch with his people already."

May Wong said: "He has not received any mail on the company since the Korean incident. That I do know. And from a source within the Air Captains Club I'm told he intends to stay on in Japan. He's shacked up with a young Japanese woman called Kimuko." She turned to King. "I think you should have him in and sort it out."

King stirred, "Not me Sugar Plum. I'm going to leave it to you and Babs Howton. Period!"

Dawson and the crew had just returned from a week of charter work between Kagoshima and Okinawa and were standing under the wing of a DC6 holding a post-mortem on the port outer engine.

"What do you think, David?" Dawson asked the flight engineer.

Chepstow came from Dorking in Surrey. He'd worked his way up from a bench fitter whilst employed by a British independent airline and managed to qualify as a flight engineer before the recession set in. He moved across the ocean to America in the hope of improving his prospects and flew for a spell with Western Airlines. He didn't seem to fit in with the American way of life so he worked a passage by sea to Japan where Oriental Air Freight snapped him up and never regretted it. If anyone could nurse a sick engine to its limit, it was Dave Chepstow.

"The old girl is tired, that's for certain." he said reaching up and patting the oil-streaked, scorched engine cowling. "She's well through her second time around and, in all fairness, she should be changed."

Chin, the Burmese co-pilot, had great difficulty in pronouncing his Ks. "I agree, slipper. She has no power and burn as much oil as she do fuel."

"How long will it take to be changed?" Dawson asked.

"Providing we got a replacement in stock it shouldn't take more than twelve hours. Kelly will probably say six."

Dawson said, "Ignore him. Tell operations the aeroplane is not available for the next twenty-four hours. It's as simple as that. And if anyone wants to moan about it they can contact me at home. I am not taking that aeroplane aloft again until the engine is changed. Is that understood?"

"Yes, boss."

"Here – here, slipper." Chin added.

Dawson relived the conversation and the long flight home that day with the sick engine, as Kimuko bathed him. It formed part of the ritual to welcome him home. He always phoned her prior to leaving the airport.

But there was something missing today; she wasn't her usual warm, enthusiastic self. She was unusually reticent and her hands moved over him with sponge and soap through a sense of duty rather than affection. She pushed him beneath the water to rinse him off.

"Is something troubling you, Kim?" he inquired when he clambered up the steps of the sunken bath to receive his robe from her.

She avoided the question and said, "Please you come and let me tweat yow face."

He lay prone upon a futon and she knelt by his head and with deft, delicate movements of a razor she shaved the hair between the scars on his face. He considered the possibility that she had tired of their relationship and the manner in which they conducted it. Or, perhaps, she had decided that a European partner was not in keeping with the tradition and culture of the Orient. Might it be he had kept her waiting too long?

She completed the shaving and treated the unscarred patches of skin with a cleansing and moisturising cream. After which she lay medicated seaweed poultices on the scars that had ruptured and were weeping. He worked too many hours to give them the attention and treatment they deserved. He looked up at her and saw sadness lurking in her eyes. Never before had he seen her so serious – so downcast. Never before had he felt so remote from her.

On finishing the treatment she handed him a mirror to inspect his face. As he did so he noticed her hand came as cold as marble to the touch. She turned her head to avoid him looking at her.

"You must tell me what is troubling you, Kim." he said and gently turned her head so that their eyes met. A tear trickled down her cheeks – followed slowly by another – and another. She started to tremble and then it totally consumed her. "Oh Gweg!" she threw herself upon him and began to weep as a distraught child.

She hid her face on his chest. He ran a hand through her hair in an attempt to soothe her whilst allowing the emotion to run its course.

After a time she calmed down a little and raised her head to look at him with a tear-stained face. "It is I am in love with you, Gweg. So velly much in love." she said hoarsely and lowered her face to his chest again.

He continued stroking her hair. "And I am very much in love with you. Have I not told you many times."

She raised her head, drew a deep breath, shuddered, and blurted out, "But you must not love me! You have wife and child in England."

He did not answer; could not answer.

"It is true, yes?"

He nodded conscious that he had brought a great injustice into her simple but well-regulated and honest world. She gave so much in life to her mother and to him and expected so little in return. Above all she deserved respect. And he had failed her miserably.

"Why you not tell me? Why you let May Wong and Bawbawa Howton come fwom company and tell me. It make me feel so fooleesh, you understand."

He had never told her how he came by the scars on his face and the long one that swept from beneath his right ear down over his shoulders to the base of his spine. She had never inquired. But he told her now, launching into the full story of his flight to Korea with Bob Holmes, his imprisonment, and his time on the run after his escape.

She never let him finish. She said, "Is it possible to forget wife and child?"

He avoided the question by saying, "Have your feelings for me changed now that you know I have a wife and child?"

She patted his hand gently in a mock reprimand, "You think I stop loving you so quick. It is not easy. You go to England and let the twuth be known, yes?"

"I could more easily send a telegram or letter."

She shook her head slowly in disapproval.

He said: "You want me to return to England to see if I am still in love with Karen. That's what it is, isn't it?"

"It is possible Karen love you more. If it were so I think you stay to be kind. Yes?"

He did not comment. Suddenly the enormity and burdensome responsibility of what she was requesting threatened to overwhelm him.

Kimuko eyed him sympathetically; "I have made you happy in our life together. Yes?

"Very happy."

"Please you go to England, to tell the twuth. It make me most happy."

Ten

The image of Kimuko faded and he found himself looking through a window of the derelict clubhouse at the rising sun. Its rays came slanting through the window painting the cobwebs silver, and drawing attention to the furniture submerged beneath a thick layer of dust. He roused himself; there was nothing he could do to restore life in the airfield. It would undoubtedly pass into oblivion and would only be remembered by those who had worked or flown from there. Perhaps, from time to time, over the years, a historian interested in aviation would remind the locals of what had been.

He took a last look in the locker room at Ron Garret's name and walked outside, across the tarmac apron to the grass beyond. He stood, smoking a cigarette, partly amused, partly serious, as he relived the flight he'd made from here as a boy. The sound of the racing Gipsy Major engine, the erratic kicking at the rudder bar to stop the nose swinging, the romping take-off. Getting into the air, climbing and turning out over the small electricity sub-station. Even at that early stage in the flight he was holding his breath and feeling tense. He turned and looked at the distant mound of Boxers' Hill. That's where he turned onto the downwind leg, he recalled. He remembered looking down the tapered wing as he banked and thinking how magical it all was. Moments later the magic turned into a nightmare when he crossed over the airfield boundary and the ground came up at him in a rush. He pulled the stick back to stop the Chipmunk diving into the ground. Then he was rising and the ground dropped out of his reach. In the next instant it raced back up to him. He closed his eyes and waited. A tremendous jolt and he thought he was climbing. A pause. Another heavy lurch, he heard metal buckle and scream as it ripped and tore. He remembered bracing his hands and arms against the buffer strip and keeping his eyes closed until the Chipmunk slithered to a halt.

He walked back across the airfield noticing how the dew sparkled like a sea of silver beads in the growing sunlight. It also reminded him of the old days when the airfield produced a healthy crop of mushrooms. He pondered on what his destiny might have been had he not wrecked the Chipmunk, and moved south. Where might he have ended up? Still living in the north amongst a people he did not understand and with whom he had so little in common?

He decided his theft of the Chipmunk had proved to be a blessing in disguise. In that it had led to a welcome change of direction in his life: the move south and his training as a commercial pilot at a prestigious flying establishment, Air Service Training Ltd., financed by persons unknown. To whom he would be eternally grateful, and who he would dearly like to thank. It disappointed him deeply to think he might easily go to his grave and never know.

He reached his car, took a last look at the dilapidated hangar and clubhouse, and drove back into the town, to the street of his boyhood. Very little, if anything, had changed. The same old terraced houses huddled together on each side of the street and reminded him, as they always had, of an army of soldiers defeated in battle. Wisps of smoke drifted from a number of chimney pots and a pall of grimy mist choked the sunlight. A dog darted from a doorway and hounded down the cobbled street. An old lady struggled up the hill in the opposite direction with a bag of shopping. It seemed the street was always in mourning; everyone dressed in black clothes.

On reaching number 46 he sat for a time preparing himself. He hadn't kept in touch with his folks after moving south. And being northerners they'd probably be quite blunt and close the door in his face. He couldn't really blame them.

The door opened to a young woman wearing a scarf fashioned as a turban, and with a cigarette wedged in the corner of her mouth.

"I'm sorry," he said. "I thought Mr and Mrs Dawson lived here."

"Not anymore." the cigarette jerked in her lips. "Her old man kicked the bucket. And she moved away. To Kinkley, I think."

"My apologies for troubling you." he said, added his thanks, and returned to the car where he was about to open the door when a harsh voice shouted:

"You should be ashamed of yourself, lad!"

He turned to find a woman standing in the open doorway of a neighbouring house. He recognised her as one of the many who came to the house to drink tea and gossip with his mother when he was a boy.

"They did a lot for you." she continued. "But what did you ever do for them. Nothing! You couldn't even bother to send them a letter or a Christmas card. I always told Mrs Dawson you'd turn out to be a right little snob." she paused to catch her breath. "There's the old man six foot under and her dying of cancer..." he let her prattle on thinking it might help her to get it off her mind...

"Do you know or care that he paid off some of that damage you did to the plane down at flying club. Heaven knows why! You weren't their boy anyway...."

Dawson felt his ears prick up and his mind was suddenly focused.

"You were abandoned and left at an orphanage with a note, amongst a lot of other unwanted war babbies. And by eck Mr and Mrs Dawson had to pick you of all the babbies out of the bunch. I bet any of the others would have been more grateful to them than you, you miserable rat."

He should have felt hurt by the revelation of his origins. Instead he felt relieved, almost elated. It explained the diffidence and strained relations he suffered all the time he lived in the north as a boy and which had not diminished over the years. The woman carried on slamming him. But he ignored her; she had told him all he wanted to know. He got into the car, let the brake off and coasted to the bottom of the street before he switched the ignition on, selected gear and let the clutch out.

He turned the corner and drove up a long sweeping road for a couple of miles and came to a number of detached properties of superior quality. In one of which his old piano tutor, Miss Methuen, resided. Wherever he'd travelled in the world he had sent her a postcard. She'd not been able to reply because he left no forwarding address.

When she opened the door to him her face lit up, tears came to her eyes and she wrapped her arms around him, "My little Frankie!" she cried. "My little Frankie." She smothered him with kisses.

She had called him Frankie from the day he started his piano lessons. And he had never challenged or questioned her on the choice of name.

She led him through the hall of her home to the sitting room and stood inspecting him. And before she could comment on his scarred face he said: "I got them during a flying accident."

"Come and sit down, Frankie. You could do with a decent breakfast. Then we'll talk."

He did feel tired and hungry; he'd had little sleep, having driven for most of the night and then sat for a long time at the airfield in the cold, damp clubhouse. A good old English breakfast would certainly not go amiss.

And the charitable Miss Methuen did not fail him. It came on a steak plate: bacon, egg, fried bread, grilled tomato, mushrooms and black pudding followed by toast and marmalade and a mug of hot sweet tea.

It revived him and she allowed him to smoke a cigarette whilst he told her the reasons for his visit to England and what had ensued: Karen's remarriage and, most recently, the disclosure about his origins.

She took his hand, and led him through to a small sitting room, which also doubled as the music room. There was the piano on which he'd learnt his music and on top stood the metronome that he had used for his timing. Nothing had changed. The same wallpaper, the same cream coloured picture rails, the same design on the curtains, the same leather chairs and settee, the same cheerful fire burning in the small grate. She seated him on the settee and sat beside him. "What did these people tell you, Frankie?"

"Not a lot, really. Basically that Mr and Mrs Dawson were not my parents. Oh, and that I came from an orphanage."

Mrs Methuen said, "I do know something about it. Are you sure you want to hear it?"

He nodded to her to carry on.

She sat back on the settee and looked out at a point in an opposite corner of the room.

Eleven

Her name was Alice, the youngest in a family of two girls and two boys. They lived in modest comfort, their father, a civil engineer, and a mother who dedicated herself to running a caring and comfortable home and raising the children. The parents put an emphasis on their early education and had ambitions for all the children to go on to University.

Alice, however, was not so inclined. She went through the motions of taking ballet lessons and learning the piano from the age of seven much as other girls in her social class did. But when she reached her teen years her interests turned to religion and nursing with the Red Cross. After leaving school she went and trained as a nurse at St. Mary's hospital in London. Then shortly after she qualified, much to her parents' amazement and against her mother's wishes, she joined the sisterhood of nuns.

She spent six months as a Postulant before being selected and formally clothed in her habit. She went on to serve two years as a novice and had made her first vows when her superiors, in consideration of her being a qualified nurse, sent her on missionary work in Africa. Where her spiritual healing and nursing skills were used in a nearby Leper Colony in addition to her main objective which was to convert local tribes to the Christian faith. Her mother tried desperately to get her to change her mind.

"Are you telling me, Alice?" she repeatedly said. "That you are prepared to give up everything? Your heart, your soul, your very life to this movement of women who deprives themselves of all the pleasures, the passion and the joy that go with the honor and privilege of womanhood."

And Alice repeatedly said, "I don't think you quite understand, mother. I have never felt the sort of passion or the joy you speak of. My joy comes through prayer and from my ability to nurse the sick and infirm and helping those who are less fortunate than me. It's a vocation, mother. I've been called to do what I'm doing. That's the way I see it."

"But have you never thought about marriage and raising a family?"

"It has never crossed my mind."

And so it came to pass that Alice set sail on a three week passage by sea, followed by a two week journey over land, travelling by oxen and cart, to reach the missionary settlement set up close to a Leper colony in the isolation and wastes of deepest Africa. She wrote every week to her parents. But her sorely disappointed parents rarely replied to her letters more than once a month.

During her stay Alice was rather amused to discover that she had inherited a number of skills from her civil engineer father. She designed and local natives helped her construct a hut some two hundred yards away from the main missionary, church and hospital. It was a single story building of wood framed walls packed with mud and clay, a grass roof, and flooring made from cattle dung packed down hard, allowed to dry out, and then polished with water. She added a veranda on the West Side.

The building consisted of a living room furnished with a table and two chairs made from wood and straw. This was divided from a small bedroom by portable hinged screens made from animal skins. Her bed consisted of a wooden frame on legs within which string netting, tightly bound, served as her mattress. Alongside the bed was a table that portrayed a Bible, a glass tumbler and jug of water, and an oil lamp. A mosquito net, in the shape of a ridge tent covered the bed and table. Above the head end of her bed there hung a simple wooden cross.

She allowed herself to indulge in one other little luxury, again of her design, and that was a shower arrangement. Oxen and cart transported a fifty-gallon anodised water tank from Bollowonga fifty miles away, bringing with it a twenty-foot length of rubber hose and a watering can.

The natives helped her set the tank up on four stilts, fifteen foot in height. A ladder of crude design was fixed to a side of the tank and natives filled the tank by collecting water from a water hole that one of them had discovered with the aid of a Witch Doctor. A deep hole had been dug at a certain spot. The hole had grown into a spring, and then, much to the surprise of the natives and the delight of the Witch doctor, into a constant large puddle of water. And when the rains came, into a small lake. They carried canvas buckets of water from the mission to Alice's tank once a week.

One end of the hose was clipped into the tank and the other end rested on a wooden fork branch driven in the ground and was within reach.

Alice operated the shower by removing the hose from the forked support and then sucking on the end to start the flow of water. On removing her mouth the water continued flowing under the force of gravity. She attached the spray head of the watering can to the hose and thus perfected her luxury of a shower.

In the six years she spent at the missionary six nuns contacted Leprosy and died. It reached a point where her superiors decided not to risk any more lives. And Alice was put in charge of the three remaining nuns who were all African converts. She gained the rather dubious distinction of being the only white woman serving in the region. The only other white person she occasionally met was a white German doctor practicing in the area who was known to be experimenting on the Lepers with a range and variety of drugs and medicines in an attempt to cure the poor souls of their debilitating disease. But like all pioneering work the path into the unknown was strewn with obstacles and hazards and many of Doctor Grubelstreichter's guinea pig subjects passed away in premature, squalid deaths.

Alice concentrated her energies on spiritual healing, the laying on of hands, and combined it with prayer in an attempt to purge the souls of the lepers and relieve them of their pain and suffering. She was not so successful in sparing them from death. But those who did pass away died peacefully holding her hand. The small number that did survive and were miraculously cured she thought they did so because of their stamina and determination rather than from the result of her prayers and healing powers.

It was Alice's innocence and lack of experience with relationships of an intimate nature that made her blind to the doctor's penchant for the young black African girls with whom he sought solace and compensation for the failure of his medical experiments.

Not until much later in her life did she really get to understand how these young girls got pregnant so early. And even more perplexing and puzzling for her was the succession of coloured, rather than black, children they produced. At no time did she connect the German doctor with the offspring of the young black mothers.

It was an hour after noon and Alice did, what she normally did each day, and that was to sit in her chair in the shade of the verandah and rest awhile. In Africa she was seldom seen in her habit. She dressed in a muslin ankle-length gown and wore a wide floppy brimmed hat that she used as a fan to cool her face and to ward off insects when sitting in the shade. In certain shades of light, unbeknown to her, she revealed that she wore lace-trimmed modesty bands around her thighs and over her breasts as undergarments.

She closed her eyes and occasionally had to swipe away a pestering fly that was attracted to tiny globules of perspiration that gathered on her neck, just beneath her chin. They were rather large flies and could give a harsh nip. So it was important they were swiped away swiftly.

She was sweeping a fifth fly off her nose with the hat when her ears detected a strange droning sound. She'd not heard anything like it before. It sounded as if it was coming from the sky, about twenty degrees above the horizon. She screwed up her eyes in an attempt to spot what it was. All she saw were vultures circling over a spot some five miles away, waiting in the queue of the food chain. Or they were simply showing a little dignity in letting the doomed beast take its last breath before they descended upon the scene.

She was pondering on what might be causing the droning when she noticed it was drawing closer and increasing in volume. She warded off another fly and moved to the veranda rail. The sun, just past its zenith, was unbearably hot. Foliage withered in the blazing heat. Sun-baked soil crumbled into dust. And the blistering heat evaporated exposed areas of water.

The droning suddenly revealed itself as an aeroplane as it came to view through the haze. It must have been about the fifth as such that she had ever seen in her life. It was the first she had seen in Africa. It reached the Missionary building and circled overhead, a single wing machine, deep red in colour, with a round-like engine at the nose of its body. As it sank lower and put its wheels down the engine noise grew louder when it approached the mission, and Alice found the hairs on the nape of her neck rising. She had never been so close before. It was incredibly exciting as it came swooping down to land. Who might it be carrying, she wondered? And what really warranted its visit to such a humble and isolated spot in the wilderness?

It struck ground with a hollow, booming sound. Then came rumbling and lurching along the arid, uneven ground pursued by a cloud of dust. It rolled to a halt just past her, swung round with a burst of engine and came back and braked perhaps a dozen yards from the veranda. The engine spluttered and clanked into silence. The dust settled and a hatch at the rear of the machine opened. An airman emerged from the hatch and went to the front of the machine and draped a sheet of material over the Perspex windows of the cockpit as a form of shading from the heat and glare of the sun. He left the rear hatch open but arranged piece of fine netting in the opening, presumably to prevent the intrusion of snakes or other inquisitive wild life.

He began to walk towards her and she took in his light brown cotton trousers, desert boots and a safari jacket, in the collar of which he used a muffler as a sweat rag. He protected his eyes with sun spectacles. His figure wavered from head to toe caught, as it was, in the mirage effect of the heat currents spiralling up around him. As he drew closer she spotted the sweat patches in the area of his armpits, on his chest and lower torso. The sight seized on her more primitive and basic instincts that had never confronted her before. Her spiritual beliefs and practices were assailed by needs of a physical nature. She felt stirrings and awakenings in her body that made her feverish and unusually excited. She had a most bizarre desire to expose herself to this beautiful, handsome aviator bearing down on her. It was the first white British male she had seen in six years.

Her imagination reached beneath his clothing. She admired the graceful movement of his limbs, his broad manly chest, and lower down the pitching and swaying motion of the prominent fruits of his masculinity. Her duty to her religion and her desires for this man clashed again and again, and caused her great anguish and frustration. Her mother's words came back to haunt her. And if her mother were to see her now, how pathetic and ridiculous she must look, trembling, and lusting after the body of this airman she had never met before.

"Oh my God!" she murmured. "And get thee hence, Satan!" she shouted through clenched teeth.

The airman jumped up the steps of the veranda, "Good afternoon Sister. I'm Bertram Hooper. I've been sent by your people at Bollowonga."

She invited him in to the shade of the veranda and to a seat. "Would you care for lemon tea?" she said. He thanked her, removed his sunglasses and used his muffler to wipe his neck and face.

The distraction of preparing the tea for him, inside the hut, came as a relief to her. It allowed her time to compose herself. She bathed her face in water and washed and dried her sweaty hands. She poured water from a kettle that was permanently left out in the sun, into a china teapot. And into each of the cups she put a slice of lemon and a spoonful of sugar.

When she returned to the veranda his eyes were closed. But he opened them when she put the tray on the table. "I hope I didn't disturb you," she said.

"Not at all. I was just resting my eyes."

"We all take an afternoon nap, here." she smiled. "Including the animals. They find a bit of shade. And off they go."

He tasted the tea and complimented her for it. He consumed a second cup in much the same time and said, "Do you mind if I smoke?"

"Not at all. But don't throw your match into the bush. It'll set us all alight."

He lighted the cigarette, extinguished the lighted match by wetting his thumb and index finger with his tongue and clamping the flame. "I've come here to tell you that Britain is at war with Germany," he said. "Your superiors think you might want to return home to be close to your relations. And because there is quite a big population of Germans here in this part of Africa, our people think there could be trouble"

"How long has the war been going on?"

"I'm not sure. But I do know the Germans have bombed London."

Alice said, "That probably explains why I haven't heard from my parents for what must be three months or more."

The airman swiped a fly away with his muffler. "So, what do you want to do?"

Alice said: "What are they intending to do in Bollowonga?"

"They are sending all the white sisters home by sea. And if you decide to go I am to fly you to the port at Mombassa."

Alice turned to him, "What do you intend to do Bertram? I mean, will it be safe for you to remain here?"

"As a matter of fact I'm on standby to fly members of the British Administration to South Africa. I don't know when that will be. It all depends on how the Germans, here, react to their superiors in Germany"

Alice got up and leaned against the veranda rail facing him. "I don't know what to say, Bertram. It puts me in bit of a quandary. I think it's rather unfair of me to just walk out on these people at a time like this. I need time to think it over."

He got up and crossed to her and took her hands, which she found strangely comforting and a novel experience; she'd never held hands with a man before.

"Look sister…"

"Please call me Alice." she interrupted. "At least when we are alone."

"Look, Alice," he smiled down at her. She suddenly felt vulnerable to his closeness and the penetrating look in his eyes. She grew weak at the knees and had to hold on to his arms for support. But she did it so tactfully he didn't really notice. Or, if he did, he ignored it to spare her from embarrassment.

"You don't have to make a decision yet," he said gently. " But they will want to know within a week. I'll fly back in a week's time."

"You mean it will be another week before I see you?" she found herself complaining. (What are you doing? What are you saying! A voice cried out in her head. Have your forgotten your vows!)

The pilot said: "I'm on my way to Barotoga to pick up a British family who want to go home. I'm to fly them to the port at Dar Es Salam. Then I go back to Bollowonga to do some courier work for a few days. I should be back here a week today."

"Then go swiftly, and take care," she whispered.

"You too, Alice," He kissed her lightly on a cheek, squeezed her hand in farewell and walked to the aeroplane. She watched him clamber in after he'd removed the shade and netting. The big radial engine started with a roar and started the ground trembling beneath her feet, and the blast from the propeller created a small dust storm. He put out a hand and waved to her. Within minutes he was at the end of a clear strip of land. He paused for a moment longer. Then turned back in her direction – hesitated – the engine note rose dramatically – and the crimson coloured, single engine monoplane came charging along the strip with the pursuing cloud of dust thinning out as it accelerated. It dashed past the veranda at full power. A hundred yards hence there came that magical moment when it left the ground and winged in to the emptiness of the sky.

She was at the hut when he returned the following week. Her heart picked up a beat at the sound of his aeroplane as it approached unseen in the heat haze. She fought to control her emotions; she had hardly slept all week. She had lain awake most nights aching for his company, agonising over her thoughts and feelings that were continually in conflict. She badly wanted to see him and, yet, the nun part of her reminded her of her dedication and the oath she had made to the Lord and the Church. She had literally prayed and asked for guidance and relief from her conflict of emotions. But her feelings for the airman had refused to away.

The aeroplane emerged from the haze with the sunlight glittering on its cockpit windscreen. It drew closer, moved overhead, and swung around in a loose turn which it continued and dropped slowly out of the air and landed, kicking up a cloud of dust as it did so. Now she was trembling, wringing her hands, smiling broadly and fighting to retain her dignity. It had never occurred to her how powerful the allure of a man could be. Betram drew her to him like a powerful magnet. The words of her mother, all those years ago, came back to haunt her repeatedly.

He waved to her from an open cockpit window when the engine lapsed into silence and the propeller juddered to a halt. In the distance, beyond the aeroplane, she noticed a number of Vultures were up and circling.

After fixing the shade and the door net to his machine Bertram strode towards her, grinning from behind his sun spectacles. The sweat patches were visible and he had a revolver secured in a holster at his waist. He took the three steps up to the veranda in one stride and took both her hands in greeting.

They were sitting, taking tea and chatting when the sky turned heavy and black. Large spots of rain began to fall and heralded the worst storm that Alice had ever witnessed or experienced. The pilot hurried back to the machine and closed the rear hatch. The rain became a torrent accompanied by booming rolls of thunder and sheets and great forks of lightning that fractured and ripped the fabric of the sky apart and defaced it like a valuable painting. The thunder continued its relentless protest. Bolts of lightning became more vivid, more frightening. The smell of ozone grew stronger. And the rain flooded the earth.

It reached the level of the veranda floor and the pilot noticed with a measure of alarm that it had reached the wheel axles of the Courier. Water started to drip from the interior of the grass roof. Alice led him to the window on the back of the hut and they could see her shower tank overflowing with the deluge of water. From the bedroom window she could not quite believe what she saw. The wooden building of the mission station had collapsed like a pack of cards and she was certain she saw steam or smoke rising from the ruins. She badly wanted to find out how her sister nuns had fared. But the fury of the storm, enraged as it was by a ferocious wind, deterred her.

The grass roof began to sag under the weight of the water. Moments later they were forced to step aside as the roof caved in and fell to the floor. The pursuing volume of water drenched them "We'd better head for the aeroplane." the pilot shouted and took her hand. "It's the only shelter left from what I see." He did not tell her the machine was being endangered by the flood waters, which had risen above the tops of the wheels. He also thought it urgent to get to the machine and block up the air intake and the exhaust manifold to prevent water getting in and ruining the engine.

Alice fetched dry clothes from a trunk beneath her bed and bundled them in a cotton bed sheet. They waded, rather than walked, to the crimson coloured Courier. Betram unlatched the door and helped her clamber inside. He got her to hand him an old oily rag from inside the machine. And taking his muffler with him he waded through the water to the front of the Courier, he stuffed the muffler up the exhaust pipe and used the oily rag as a bung in the air intake of the engine.

Alice's first impression of the interior of the Courier was that it was rather cramped and smelt rather strangely. Bertram told her later that it was all part of an aeroplane's character, the drift of fuel fumes, the oil from the engine, the smell of the leather seats and the special acid-drop paint used on the inside of the cabin. He squeezed past her and folded up five seats giving them more room. From the back of the cabin he opened a small hatch cover, took out a towel and handed it to her. "I'll nip up front so that you can change into dry clothes," he said.

"You can't do that, Bertram. I need your help to get my dress off. It's stuck to me with the rain water."

He began by dragging the sodden linen up from her ankles. It got caught up at her waist and he was forced to open his eyes. And what he saw was something quite breathtaking.

"If you push the dress higher up my back I'll pull it off, over my head." she said. And as he did so he grew very aware of her naked gleaming, white form and the roundness of her thighs and narrow waist. He could count the gentle impressions of the vertebrae of her narrow back and he admired the gentle slope of her shoulders.

"That's it!" she called as she pulled the soaking dress over her head and it flopped to the floor, causing a small puddle of water. Her wet, shining body gave off a musky scent much like that of grass after a fall of rain. He dried her down by gently patting the towel on her naked form from her slender neck to her delicate ankles.

He was not quite prepared for what she did next. She turned around and honoured him with a full frontal view of her body. It was the first time in his life he had witnessed a naked woman and he felt shocked and somewhat intrigued that it should be that of a nun.

He likened the marble form and texture of her body to the work of a sculptor. The curves of her shoulders, the tilt of her bust, the arcs of the creases at her armpits, it was artistically and delightfully carved. As was the shape and prominence of her breasts whose summits exhibited a distinctive deep red cherry; he had never seen anything quite so spectacular, so beautiful, and so desirable. He froze again in admiration of all that she portrayed.

Alice said, "Don't you think it's time you got out of your wet clothes, Bertram?"

She undid his muffler and the buttons of his safari jacket and pushed it back over his shoulders where it slid down his arms to the floor. She touched him in admiration of his manly chest and was aroused by the scent of his damp body. The thunder continued to boom, the lightning crackled ferociously, the rain lashed the outside of the wooden aeroplane and the gusting antics of the wind had occasion to rock the Courier. And carried by the momentum and passion of the storm Alice laid down on a narrow strip of carpet that lined the cabin floor between the passenger seats and invited him to take possession of her.

He lowered himself gently onto her and began thrusting and retreating to a strict tempo. She sensed rather than knew that the pain and the initial resistance to his entry was all part of the deflowering process and would ultimately reward her with the fullness of a woman.

During a long roll of thunder, frequent bolts of lightning, torrential rain and a howling wind, the storm reached its climax and, as it did so, he pierced the tissue that removed her virginity and gave her the mantle of a woman. She arched her back and spread her legs to aid deeper penetration, closed her eyes, and cried out at the intensity of the pain, and joy, that overwhelmed her.

Mysteriously the pain disappeared and his frantic movements upon her, and within her, and her feverish responses had her surging along on a wave of intoxication that she had never experienced before. It came to her as a sheer and uninterrupted bliss, an intense hunger satisfied. She became ecstatic and free, and wished it would go on and never end.

But end it did forced, as it was, by the exhaustion of their passions and the gratification of their desires. They lapsed, exhausted, into sleep almost at the same time as the fury of the storm abated, the skies cleared, and day turned into night.

"Are you telling me I was conceived in an aeroplane?" Dawson broke in on Mrs Methuen's tale.

"It would appear so, Frankie."

" I suppose that's where I get the bug for flying? From the genes of Betram?"

Mrs Methuen nodded, "Very possible."

"Where do I get the liking for the piano from?"

"I told you earlier that your mother learnt the piano as a girl."

"Ah, so you did."

"She continued playing the piano with the nuns and also mastered the organ at the mission station in Africa. She played it at all the Sunday services."

Dawson lit another cigarette and blew a stream of smoke toward the ceiling of the room. "It's amazing isn't it. I'm stuck up here all those years, not feeling particularly happy with my lot, amongst people I can't relate to. And all the time I'm the son of an aviator and a musical nun. Quite a pedigree isn't it?" He turned to his old piano tutor. "What made them abandon me? How did I come to end up here from my conception in the African bush?"

Mrs Methuen continued:

"Alice awoke first next morning to a calm day. Sunlight poured through the cabin windows and the growing heat stirred the odours left over from their moments of passion. She disentangled herself from Bertram by gently removing his arm from around her neck and lifting one of his legs that was draped over her thighs. It was growing incredibly hot in the cabin. She opened the cabin door, grateful for the relatively cooler, fresher air that entered. She slipped into an ankle-length cotton undergarment and took her and Bertram's wet clothes and put them out to dry, by spreading them across the tailplane and fuselage of the Courier.

She made her way to the hut to find that after the roof caved in the building imploded. She found a small crevice where a collapsed wall leant against a section that remained intact and after some careful rummaging she found her washing bag and a towel. In Bertram's absence she toileted and took a shower. She smiled at the shower tank stood upon its four stilts, perhaps leaning a little but had survived the pressures of the storm. And it stilled functioned. She lathered her body with soap and later enjoyed the luxury of rinsing off with the soft rain water left over in the tank from the storm. She came out of the wooden cubicle and spotted Bertram approaching, dressed in shorts, bush hat and carrying a towel and small bag. "Good morning," he said enthusiastically. "May I use your shower."

"But, of course. It looks to be the only thing left standing."

"Have you been up to the Mission yet? It doesn't look too good."

"I'd rather you came with me."

He went and had a shower. And she took a canvas bucket of water and cleaned the interior of his aeroplane and removed the red stains marking the carpet on which she had surrendered her virginity.

Later when she and Bertram walked to the main part of the Mission they discovered that the only building to escape the wrath of the storm was the small wooden chapel in which they found the discarded habits of the African nuns. Alice screwed her face up in thinking the worse. She led the way out of the chapel when Pippit, an African boy, who she had adopted when his Leper parents died, confronted her. He always wore a startled expression that clearly showed the whites of his eyes, and he walked with a limp, due to a leg being shorter than the other did till she designed and fitted him with a club boot. She drew him to her, "Where is everybody, Pippit?"

"They is dead sizzie."

"Whose dead?"

"The dockie, the lepees. And the Voodoo man. They is struck down by lightning. They is all burn. No more nasty sickees."

"What happened to the sisters in the Mission?"

"They is not dead. They is go home."

"Home!"

"They is back in the bush with their people. They say storm tell them go back home."

Bertram moved up behind her and rested his hands on her shoulders, "What's he saying?"

"He claims Doctor Grubelstreichter and the local Witch doctor have been struck down and killed by lightning. And so have all the Lepers. And my sister nuns have returned to their tribe."

He squeezed her shoulders, "I truly am sorry for you Alice. This must be a terrible blow to you after all the work you have put in over the years."

She reached up and put a hand on his. "Strange as it may seem, Bertram, but I think it's happened because God has willed it so. There are various passages in the Bible which quotes the casting out of sin and pestilence, and other ills of mankind."

Bertram said, "A very ruthless way of doing it, if I may say. I thought our God was a compassionate and understanding being."

Alice avoided getting into a discussion on the matter. She got Pipit to take them on a tour of the devastation. The two-mile square area of the Leper Colony had been burnt and flattened. It represented nothing more than a black landscape with occasional small heaps to suggest where a mud and straw home had once been. There were no signs of the remains of the Lepers, only a light grey ash dotted here and there. They found no bones.

At Alice's request Pippit lead them to the native settlement, which was a mile in the opposite direction from the Mission. The sun shone with a great heat and brilliance and she noticed that the bush around them had turned a luscious green after the torrential rain. Pipit walked in front. She took the liberty to put an arm through that of Bertram. She felt unreasonably happy. Or was it a great joy? For certain she had not ever felt so exhilarated. She felt vibrant, vital, as if the world belonged to her. It coursed through her veins like a river. She loved Bertram deeply but could not really explain why.

She broke away from him as they approached the cluster of mud and straw huts and two of the inhabitants with painted faces and carrying a shield and spear confronted them.

"I wish to speak to Marisus, Cogolese and Jangalet," she said.

One of the natives thrust his shield forward and threatened her with the spear. "You go! They stay with friends in tribe. They not want you. You bring storm. It kill many people."

Alice made an attempt to reason with the native but his friend acted in the same way with his shield and spear. "This not your country, and our people are not your people. You bring trouble and strife. You go!"

"But you don't understand." Alice appealed and was about to step forward gesturing with her hands when Bertram gripped her by the shoulders and checked her. "Don't do it, Alice," he said in a low voice. "They're not in the mood for negotiating. Thank them and we'll beat a diplomatic retreat. Walk backwards for the first ten paces in case they decide to launch a spear."

Safely back near the Courier Bertram told her it would be prudent for her not to delay her departure from the area. She insisted they have a meal and got Pippit lighting a fire and she dug out some tinned food from amongst the ruins of the missionary. She also found some dried meat and in a cooler box the remains of a Skidgy, an animal whose meat tasted something like a mixture of deer and goat and was common only to this part of Africa. The colour and texture of the meat resembled that of venison.

Bertram also brought tinned sausages and beans, and tinned fruit from the Courier. They formed part of the emergency kit should he be forced down in a remote area by a mechanical problem with the Courier. They grilled the Skidgy on the fire and ate it with heated sausages and beans and used the tinned fruit for a dessert.

During the meal she told Bertram she thought they should take Pippit with them. Pippit's eyes grew larger and he waved his arms frantically. He said that he belonged to the bush and, in no way, was he going to travel in the noisy Red Devil that he called the Courier. He said he might try and rebuild the mission church for her.

Alice got her very first taste of flying when Bertram flew her out of the Mission and took her to Bollowonga. She marvelled at the large empty space of the sky in which the Courier was suspended and how slowly it seemed to travel. They circled for a while to give her a chance to have a last look at the remains of the mission station and the large surrounding area of scorched earth that once had accommodated the Leper colony and the German doctor's surgery. Bertram also took her over the cluster of mud and straw huts where the African nuns had retreated. None of the natives came out to watch the orbiting Courier.

Alice found it all rather sad. She told Bertram not to bother any longer and that they should get on their way. She stood behind his seat, a hand resting on his shoulder, listening to the steady beat of the engine, and trying to navigate their progress in the limited visibility of the heat haze. Way beneath the wings she spotted a gathering of vultures circling over the scraggy remains of a beast she could not identify. Then she noticed Bertram was following a narrow straight track through a mixture of bush and scrubland. Occasionally the Courier leapt up and down and was struck a hard blow that echoed through its wooden construction.

"Heat bumps!" Bertram explained. "It comes off the sort of terrain over which we're flying. It'll disappear once the trees are gone."

Their flight became smoother once they got over level open scrubland. But it was incredibly hot in the Courier. Bertram opened both side vents and the cooler air came wafting in aided and abetted by the noisy engine and thrashing propeller. It was impossible to hold a conversation.

They flew on for a further twenty minutes and then Bertram turned his head and shouted, "We'll be landing soon. Take your seat and put the belt on, please." The engine lost its gusto of sound as he throttled back and raised the nose a little to reduce speed and lower the undercarriage and drop a few degrees of flap. She sat looking through a window, over a tilting wing. As part of the landing checks the pilot closed the side vents, shutting out the excessive noise The ground was much closer now; Alice saw an open stretch of scrub and a couple of wooden buildings, and a large yellow sock hanging at a mast. Bertram levelled the wings. The engine grew quieter and she heard the air swishing past the fuselage windows. The Courier lurched for a moment, as the pilot put on full flap, then dropped its nose and floated down with utter grace and gentleness till two solid jolts on either side of her seat told her they had landed.

Alice spent three glorious and deeply happy months in Bollowonga. Bertram proposed to her and a remaining official of the British administration married them. They set up home in Bertram's small straw-roofed clay and wood home that rested on four, four feet high stilts designed to deter rats and snakes and other curious wild life. But their biggest deterrent was a raccoon, a stealthy, ferocious animal that volunteered its services as a family pet.

Bertram was often away for days on end but each time he came back it was like another honeymoon. She did not trouble him with her worries about the lack of mail from her parents; she put it down to the war in Europe. She would have enjoyed telling her mother about the new dimension of life she was leading and about the child she was expecting, and her wonderful experience of flying in an aeroplane. She had detached herself from the sisterhood of nuns but she continued to read the bible each day and make her prayers morning and night.

Then it all drastically changed. Who or what incited it they never found out. The natives suddenly took it into their heads to rebel against the British white residents. They burned down the local church and small businesses and then started on the homes. Bertram never gave her a chance to confront the wrath of the rebels. He got her to pack a few belongings in a suitcase and took her to the airstrip and filled the Courier with fuel, put a number of cans inside the cabin, and they took to the air only minutes after the natives put a torch to their home.

With the help of a following wind and prudent use of the fuel mixture control they reached Atbara in the Sudan where they refuelled from the cans in the cabin. Alice felt Bertram should take a rest after this. But he said they must press on. He flew the Courier to the Red sea and followed the west coast northwards and they landed at Cairo. They managed to get fuel from an abandoned Imperial airways fuel dump. And to their great relief they managed to get a bath and a meal at the British Embassy who took note of their plight and also offered them a bed for the night.

The Embassy advised them against trying to fly into England. Evidently things were quite bad there. France and the Channel Islands were in German hands and their bombing raids on Britain were carried out from aerodromes in France. They suggested the couple should make for Spain and approach the British Embassy for advice.

They arrived back in Britain during an air raid on Coventry docks, after nearly a month at sea, sailing in an old Dutch barge owned and operated by a dubious but humorous Irishman, Arty O'Farty, recommended to them by the British Embassy in Spain. They had sold the Courier and used most of the money to pay for the passage in the barge.

Betram helped Arty get the sail down and start the engine. They hove to and looked at the fires raging red in the docks and casting their reflection on the sea. Further back in the city intermittent explosions were loud enough to reach their ears. "I tink you got two choices," Arty said. "I slip you in now and you'll not be noticed amongst all the mayhem. Or we wait till it calms down. But oi must be on my way before daylight."

So urgent had their flight been out of Africa and the hot, tiresome, lumpy flight to Spain they had not given a lot of thought to what they would do when they arrived in Britain. They needed money to pay for food and shelter for the night and with facilities for Alice to wash. She had not fared well at sea.

To avoid the West Coast of German-occupied France Arty headed the barge way out into the Atlantic and the notorious Bay of Biscay and then tacked back to the British Isles and to Coventry, which he considered a convenient stopping-off point on his way back to Ireland.

They had encountered storms and large running swells that had large troughs. Alice suffered miserably from seasickness. She lost her appetite and never got a full night's sleep. It had a detrimental effect on the child she was carrying but she never complained about it. Bertram, however, was only too aware that she was in urgent need of care and attention.

"We'll go ashore now, Mr O'Farty," he said. "If you look to the left, just visible on the edge of the fire there is a quay wall with steps."

"Roight now," he turned the wheel and gave the engine a touch of power. "You get below and bring your cases on deck. And I'll take her alongside."

Bertram did not bargain for the steps of the quay that spent most of their time under water, being covered in seaweed. With O'Farty holding the barge alongside with the engine he put the two suitcases on the steps and made to step ashore, slipped on the shiny seaweed and fell back on the boat. He hauled himself back up and made his way gingerly onto the concrete step. He turned about feeling vulnerable and anxious about getting the pregnant, unwell Alice ashore. He couldn't see very well; the quay wall blanked off the fires burning in the docks. The dark shape of the barge rose and fell gently before him, its timbers grating against the quay wall. Alice had great difficulty in lifting a leg onto a gunwale from which he would pull her onto the step. She almost pulled him back to the boat. Then O'Farty was there lifting and pushing her to him. "Hold her tonight moi boi," he shouted and rushed back to the wheelhouse.

Bertram got her leaning against the sea wall and told her to wait whilst he took the suitcases up the steps. He slipped a number of times on the seaweed and only just about spared himself and a case from falling into the sea. If he'd known it was going to be so treacherous he would have waited till daylight.

Helping Alice up the steps also proved to be something of a nightmare. It took her some time to get accustomed to her 'land' legs after the gruelling month at sea and she was so poor in health. She tripped and she stumbled, she sighed and she mumbled.

At last they reached the top of the steps and whilst she paused to get her breath he spotted O'Farty's barge slinking away to the north east just on the edge of the reflections in the water of the fires in the docks.

They picked their way through the fallen cranes and derricks, the demolished warehouses and passenger terminal. Fires and smoke were now visible in the city and the bells of a fire engine and ambulance could be heard. Every couple hundred yards Bertram found it necessary to stop and rest his arms; he would not let Alice touch a case.

At last they reached the city boundary. They trudged through the dark, lonely streets with water from a burst water main washing over their shoes and there was a strong smell of gas. During one of his pauses to rest his arms Alice said, "Where are we heading for, Bertram?"

"It's bit of a long shot but I'm hoping to find a Salvation Army Hostel."

"What for?"

" To get us food and shelter for the night."

Alice was so weak and tired she didn't really care where they spent the night. It was as much as she could do to lift her feet and keep her eyes open.

At that moment an Air Raid Warden came across them. "Are you from the bombed out area down near the docks?"

"That's right, Warden." Bertram said. Alice cringed behind him.

"Right," he turned and pointed up the street, "Take the second turning on your left. Then take the first turning to your right and follow that road for about half a mile and you'll come to a low set building between two tall office blocks. The small building has been set up as an Emergency Centre. You'll get food and drink. And I think they got some beds as well."

"That's very kind of you Warden. Thank you."

The warden was about to move off when he turned and said, "Did you notice any others wandering about down near the docks?"

"No. But we did notice the road was awash with water. And there was a strong smell of gas. I think the mains have gone."

"Right, thanks," he began marching up the street. "I'd better report it to the Fire Brigade and the Gas board."

Alice waited for him to get out of earshot. She smiled and said, "You fibber, Bertram. You said we lived down by the docks."

"No, I did not my dear. He asked if we were from the bombed out area of the docks. And I said we were. He did not mention anything about us living there." He picked up the cases and they plodded on through the streets as the warden had advised them.

They came to the smaller building between the office blocks, groped around in the blackout to find the entrance door, knocked on it and the door opened only a matter of inches. A voice told them to hurry, on account of the blackout precautions, and pushed the door further ajar to allow them access.

An elderly man and woman sat at a wooden table just inside the door. The man turned out to be a GP and as soon as he saw Alice he went to her, "My goodness!" he exclaimed. "Come and take a seat. I think you need to go to hospital."

Alice tried to tell him it wasn't necessary. All she needed was a bite to eat somewhere to wash and change into fresh clothing, and a place to sleep.

"You are pregnant, are you not?"

"Yes,"

"How many months?"

She had to think a bit because she so tired. "Getting on for four," she said after a long pause.

The doctor turned to Bertram, "As her husband I would advise you to tell your wife that she needs the facilities of a hospital. She is undernourished and in very poor health. She could very easily lose the child if she doesn't get treatment." He paused and added. "I'll run you to the hospital in my car, if you like."

Bertram said, "Is there somewhere you and I could speak in private?"

The doctor led him across the hall to a door that led into the wings of a curtained stage. And Bertram told him of their arrival in the country by the barge and briefly what he and Alice had done in East Africa. His concern at taking her to hospital stemmed from the fact that neither of them had an identity card and therefore could be arrested as spies.

"So what do you intend to do now?" the doctor said.

"Contact our parents. Mine live in Bristol. My wife's parents live in Surrey. I also need money for the rail fare to get down to Bristol and Surrey."

"Right! First things first. I'll get your wife into hospital, claiming she is one of my patients. Then whilst she is there you and I can chat about the money."

"I'll also need to find some accommodation, till she gets out of hospital."

"But you said you were without money?"

" I'll try and get free accommodation at a Salvation Army hostel."

The doctor said, "I think you'd better hang on here till morning. Then you can come with me when we take your wife to hospital in daylight. If we went now I'd probably run into a bomb crater or pile of rubble. In the meantime I think you should get a mug of tea and a sandwich. You don't look too clever yourself."

Immediately they arrived at the hospital in the morning a nurse took charge of Alice, after a brief conversation with the doctor, and took her immediately to have a bath. She wallowed in the luxuries of lazing in warm water and washing away the sweat, the grime and the stale smell of her body that had been enforced upon her by the confinement and the ordeal of her month at sea. She slipped between the white starched linen of the bed sheets and enjoyed their crisp feel and clean smell. She devoured a small bowl of porridge and two rounds of toast. Then she was ordered to rest and Bertram and the doctor were asked to leave, reassured that she was in good hands.

Alice slid willingly beneath the bedclothes, pulling them high around her neck, closed her eyes and drifted into oblivion, smiling.

Dawson broke into the story again. His lack of sleep the previous night was now beginning to tell. He felt weary and was losing his concentration. And without being impolite he felt Mrs Methuen was a bit slow in getting to the point. He said, "I'm sorry for interrupting Mrs M but can you tell me briefly how I ended up in the orphanage. And then with my foster parents?"

Mrs Methuen put a hand on his and looked at him with misty eyes and there was a quiver in her voice, "Your mother died, giving birth to you, Frankie. She went through a lengthy labour and delivered you to the world. And when the midwife severed the umbilical cord, cleaned you up, and laid you against your mother's breast, your mother smiled, kissed the crown of your head, uttered a loud sigh and faded away. The hospital cared for you for a number of weeks. Then like all orphans you were placed in an orphanage. You were about four or five when you were put up for fostering. That's when Mr and Mrs Dawson appeared on the scene."

"What happened to Bertram, my father?"

"As far as we know he joined the air force, after your mother passed away, and spent most of his time abroad in India flying supplies across the Hump to Burma."

Dawson blew a stream of cigarette smoke toward the ceiling of the room. "Strange isn't it," he said. "How my father was destined to work abroad. And how I have ended up doing the same. Did he ever come back after the war?"

"Briefly. He had a stone put up in Coventry cemetery in memory of your mother. It mentioned she had belonged to the sisterhood of nuns and served six years as a missionary and spiritual healer alongside a leper colony in the depths of Africa. It added that she had subsequently become the wife of Bertram Hooper, a civilian aviator, and had died giving birth to their son who was later christened Gregory."

"What happened after that?"

"He went abroad again, to Penang this time. He flew for the national airline and by all accounts married a attractive woman of that region."

Dawson frowned at her, "How did you come by all this information?"

"My brother is a solicitor. And when your father came back after the war he instructed my brother on a number of matters. They kept in touch when your father went out to Penang for reasons I did not find out until much later. And that's about as much as I know."

He put an arm around her shoulders and gave her an appreciative squeeze. "Thanks for everything you've told me. It explains a number of things that have puzzled me for years. Like why I never felt at home up her. My parents were not from these parts, were they? And whilst I got on well with you that was because you were originally from the south weren't you? Didn't you tell me once that you came from a little village in Sussex?"

She patted him with a motherly hand. " Yes, I did." She stirred. "I think it's time we had a little lunch and another pot of tea."

He followed her into her small kitchen and whilst she busied herself with the preparations of the food he sat on a stool and said, " There is only one more thing that has puzzled me, over the years, and that is: who sponsored my flying training at Air Service Training Ltd? It has troubled me for years."

"Why should it trouble you?"

" It was an extremely expensive and generous contribution to my life and I'd like the chance to thank the person or persons responsible."

The piano teacher smiled at him," Have you no idea who it was?"

He shook his head. "No idea. You see, Karen assured me it was not her and Ron Garret got killed, as you may possibly know and died with hardly a penny to his name." He paused. "At one time I thought old Barnaby, at the solicitors may have coughed up the money. He gave me my first full-time job when I moved south, you see. And he helped out again later when I was out of work, desperately trying to get into commercial flying."

"Did you actually find out if he did?"

"I never did ask him. But I don't think he did. He was keener for me to have a future in the law business. Although I must say he wished me well when I told him I wanted to go into aviation."

She said, "Has it occurred to you that your sponsor might like to remain anonymous for whatever reasons and consider your gratitude unnecessary."

"You mean they might be offended?"

"It's possible."

Hold on a moment! Dawson suddenly construed that something was not quite right. How would Mrs Methuen know it might offend them?

He turned to her smiling; "It was you Mrs M!"

"What do you mean, it was me?" she moved awkwardly beside him and she was blushing.

"You paid for my flying training. Of course, I see it all now. It could have only been you." He paused and held her with his eyes. "It was you, wasn't it?"

She took both his hands. "Not quite, Frankie. Bertram, your father, put the money in trust for you. He did it through my brother, the solicitor, and I was appointed as a trustee."

"But how did you find out where I was? The only person who knew of my move south was Ron Garret. And what was more how did you get hold of my Bank details to lodge the money?"

She said: " I read about your flying escapade in the local Herald, which read: YOUNG INTREPID AVIATOR COMES BACK TO EARTH WITH A BUMP. It quoted you by name and only mentioned the aeroplane was severely damaged.

I visited Mrs Dawson to see how you were. But she said she didn't know because you were in lodgings on the other side of Rigby. I went by bus to the address one afternoon and met," she paused and frowned.

"Mrs Clotter?" he reminded her.

"Yes. That's right. She was rather puzzled because you left at short notice and gave no forwarding address. But fortunately she remembered Mr Garret who had visited you from the club. So off to the flying club I went. And through his help and his mother in Southampton I got your Bank address and gave it to my brother to make the necessary legal arrangements. Your trust matured when you reached eighteen years of age and specified it must be used only for flying training.

TWELVE

Dawson arrived back in Japan a week later, satisfied that he had got his affairs, in England, back into some kind of order. He'd managed, after a struggle, to persuade Mrs Methuen to accept a cheque to put toward a music scholarship for one of her pupils of her choice who she thought would make the grade for a music college in London.

He'd also managed to have a lengthy conversation with Karen by telephone during which they discussed their son's future. She wanted no maintenance for herself, in return for which he would sign the house over to her. And rather than he send any money for Simon's subsistence she suggested Dawson set up a trust fund for the boy that could be paid out at the age of 21.

Everything was agreed amicably and could not have been negotiated better than by the daughter of a diplomat, as Karen was.

Tokyo International airport was seething with masses of people arriving to make their annual pilgrimage to Kami Fuji. Out of the crowd a figure leapt at him, bowed courteously and gripped his hand, "It is most pleasing to see you slipper." Chin, his co-pilot, of late, grinned broadly. Chin had still not mastered the pronunciation of his Ks.

Dawson put a hand over Chin's, "It's great to be back Chin. How is everybody?"

"They all fine. But Kimuko, she most sad. Her mother passed away shortly after you go to England. She most lonesome."

The surging crowd sucked Chin back into its current. "She come on early flight, and go to Fuji." he called out before the surging mass of people swallowed him up.

Dawson slipped his bags into the company office and took a train out to the suburbs of Fujiyama. He arrived as the daylight was fading and lanterns and burning torches illuminated the groups and processions bowing and chanting their respects to the towering Fuji.

Others who had already paid homage gathered at refreshment stalls.

Barbecues and open fires grilled meat and fish delicacies and woks and pots, burning on charcoal, cooked rice, bean shoots and other small savouries. A stall had been set up to sell saki and was attracting a wealth of customers.

Dawson made his way amongst the bantering and chanting conscious of Fujiyama towering overhead wearing a crown of sparkling stars. He scoured the eastern fringes looking for her.

After about an hour he came upon a solitary pagoda its outline marked with strings of gaily-coloured lanterns in the swooping darkness. A mixture of maple, cedar, spiced herbs, and a drift of wood smoke, hung pleasantly on the evening air.

As he came around the side of the pagoda the ground sloped away down to a small wooden, rickety bridge on which a figure in a white kimono stood gazing reverently up at the dominant spectacle of Fujiyama.

Dawson froze, unable to believe his ears. Piano music floated from the pagoda, making the hairs on the nape of his neck bristle. He recognised the music as his music – the piece he had knocked up all those years ago in England on New Year's eve'. He saw an aeroplane flying past the summit of Fuji. He saw the slit eyes and menacing faces of his interrogators. He felt the agonising burns on his face. He heard a man cry out under torture, the shrieks of a raped woman.

He saw dead bodies sprawled in the snow. He trembled and sweated in the throes of the nightmare that frequently visited, and digested, him.

Slowly the scenes began to fade taking the pain and torment with them, and were replaced by the young woman standing alone on a wooden, rickety bridge.

He moved down the slope towards the bridge whilst the piano music of his musical legend continued to tell its story, diminishing to trinkets of sound when he reached the bridge and the babbling water below reflected the glittering light of the stars. He moved up behind her and gently gripped her narrow shoulders. A soft warm hand reached up for his and for some time they stood motionless – speechless

"I think this marks the ending of the story, Kim," he said gently.

She turned slowly to face him, smiling, and cupped his face in her hands. "I think not, Greg. I think our story is about to begin."